NANCY

DIANA ELIZABETH TEBBUTT

U K Book Publishing.com

Editing, design, typesetting and publishing by UK Book Publishing

www.ukbookpublishing.com

ISBN: 978-1-916572-37-9

NANCY

I must thank Tania for her help and encouragement in writing this book.

THE VAGARIES OF LIFE

Who knows what changes life can bring,
Who knows the way that lives can swing,
Who knows what chances may come and go,
Is it better by far perhaps not to know.

Life may bring happiness, it may bring grief,
It may bring solace and much relief,
It may make us happy or make us sad,
It may make us tearful or make us glad.

We have one life, we should treasure it well,
Many experiences there will be to tell,
Savour the moments, deep within your heart,
From their memories never do part.

There will always be ups and many downs,
Treat them with laughter, never with frowns,
Welcome the commencement of each and every day,
And make the most of the part you look to play.

DEL 2023

CHAPTER 1

The cottage was small, but on the outside very pretty. Wisteria crept along the walls, but missed the latticed windows. Inside there were just two rooms downstairs, a living room and a scullery. Upstairs there were two bedrooms, one with a sloping ceiling underneath the eaves. There was a small garden at the front and one at the rear, but despite all efforts, there were many weeds. There were, however, some herbs and vegetables growing.

Mary sighed. She was so tired; her hands were swollen from the use of lye soap used in washing. She took in washing in order to make ends meet and her daughter Nancy's teaching, brought in little money. She had a job to find money for the family and clothes for the boys. She had to obtain coal for the copper and had sometimes taken out a bucket to steal coal where she could.

CHAPTER 2

Once, she had led a perfect life, the daughter of a rich merchant, Mr Wakefield, she had had lovely clothes and lived in a large red-bricked house. She had been waited upon by servants and had been spoiled and cosseted. She did have a brother, Bertram, but he was doted upon by her mother. This did not detract from the fact that her life was smooth and pleasant. She had a governess who taught her deportment, and all basic skills. Life had been good. However, her father had employed a new valet, Antonio Farran. He was charming, dark and handsome. She had fallen in love with this handsome young man and given him every encouragement. She had met him away from the house and he had taught her the art of love.

He had kissed and caressed her to the point where her body was crying out for more. They met secretly in the summer house some way away from the main house.

She would slip from her bedroom down the back stairs and he would come to her when his duties were done at night.

Antonio put his hands in her secret places, and sucked her breasts, causing her to moan with pleasure. Antonio encouraged her to put her hands on his swollen member and they had both reached the point of no return. He had removed her underclothes and shed his own clothing. He had entered her and although at first she had cried out with pain, as he gradually moved inside her the most wonderful sensation had built up inside her, and she felt the most fantastic explosion of the senses. Antonio had his release and she had felt his wetness between her thighs. After a while they had crept back to the house.

They met more frequently and Mary could not resist this newfound pleasure.

This continued for at least three months. Mary still met friends and was due for a coming out ball, but all her thoughts were on the secret meetings with Antonio.

A time elapsed. Mary could not understand her morning sickness and heavy breasts. She was so sick one morning her mother challenged her, hardly daring to guess the cause of the frequent bouts of sickness. Mary had confessed her love for Antonio almost with pride. Her mother's scream of outrage had brought her father from his study.

Mary often relived the whole dreadful scene as her father's rage had been terrible. He had sent a servant to find his valet. "How dare you violate my daughter," he thundered. "I brought you into my house and trusted you. I could throttle you with my bare hands."

Mary had cried out. "I love him. We are in love, Father. There is no one in the world that I could ever love more. Father, let us marry. Antonio is very intelligent and you could employ him in your business. The dowry I was going to have could purchase us a very respectable residence and furnish it."

"You talk nonsense, girl. Your dowry was if you made a respectable marriage. I was hoping that you might find favour with a gentleman with a title. One who could provide you with the luxuries of life. I would never, never, never employ such a snake in the grass. Someone who has abused my trust so completely. As for you, girl, you are just a common whore, you are no longer any daughter of mine."

He turned to Antonio. "Take her, but you get no money from me. I have no wish to ever see the pair of you again."

He turned back to Mary. "Girl. You have smashed all my hopes and dreams for you. What good are my riches when I have fathered such a slut. Ha! He didn't even need to pay you for your services."

Antonio had remained silent as he listened to this tirade.

Mary sobbed, "Have pity, Father, we are in love."

Her father answered, "Love, what do you know of love? Love has decency and standards. Love shows respect. What respect was there here? You must have crept out like thieves in the night, and for you, Mary, to behave like some common trollop.

Mary's mother, Georgina, at last intervened. "Husband, show some mercy to our daughter." She knelt in front of him. "Please show some mercy."

Mary's father had softened at his wife's plea. He had drawn her from her knees and said, "Very well, wife. I bought a small cottage many years ago for a game keeper before I married you and we moved here. He caught his foot in his own trap, got gangrene and died. Another couple of workers lived in it, but they caught a fever and died. I have no idea what state it is in now, but it is about five miles from here. I sold my family home after my parents died, and purchased this present house, Thornton." Her father scribbled an address. "Go there and get you both gone in the morning."

Georgina had wept and retired to her room.

Antonio suddenly spoke. "We will go now," he said. "Get your things, Mary, and we will be off."

Mary's father exploded further. "Oh, very clever." He threw some money at Antonio.

"Here are your wages, plus a little extra. See how far that will get you. Now get out."

Mary had run upstairs and thrown some things into a carpet bag. She had a little pin money left, so took this as well. They left.

With Mary's pin money they had managed to purchase a horse and cart even at that late hour, from a local farmer. They had travelled quickly through the night and after several wrong turns, found the cottage. When they found it, it was in a sorry state at a place called Merridon. The door was off its hinges, but the windows were still intact. Inside was some furniture covered in cobwebs and the floor was filthy. There were two rooms downstairs – a living room and a scullery – and two bedrooms upstairs. There were beds and cupboards, but all the bed linen had rotted.

Outside was a shed, which still had some hay and here they put the horse. They gave it water from a pump underneath in an old bucket. They also put the cart in another part of the shed which was surprisingly quite large and still intact. They had gone back into the cottage and just slept exhausted on the floor.

The next day, after eating the biscuits Mary had brought with her, Antonio set off to look for work. He was lucky, as a local farmer needed an extra hand on his farm. He and his wife had taken pity on the young couple and provided them with bread, butter, milk and more hay for the horse.

Mary had set to and cleaned the cottage. She had found cloths and cleaned the windows. She found an old broom and swept and cleaned the floor. Luckily the pump in the scullery provided water and the scullery had an old oven and copper. Antonio repaired the door and found kindling to light the stove and for the fire in the living room.

CHAPTER 3

As time progressed Mary felt happy. Her father had always been overbearing, and she had always felt that although she was well cared for, her brother Bertram was the real favourite and totally indulged. Mary and Antonio were quietly married in the village church with only the verger and church warden as witnesses.

Antonio was kind and Mary was with a man she loved. The cottage and little garden front and back were all gradually taking shape and they had grown some vegetables and herbs.

Antonio was well paid, enjoying his work with farmer Jones. They managed to purchase additional items for the cottage including new beds, chairs and tables. Mary also purchased cooking utensils.

Mary's pregnancy progressed well, but as time went on she was unable to do so much around the cottage. When her waters broke she did not understand and staggered to farmer Jones' wife. Mrs Jones and Antonio helped her home and had sent for the local midwife, Bessy Bridges. Miraculously the birth was quick, and baby Nancy was born. Mary had already purchased baby clothes from the nearby village where she shopped and Bessy Bridges had helped her to put everything in good order. Antonio had made a lovely cradle and the baby was placed inside. Mary felt so happy and Nancy was loved dearly. Antonio was receiving even more money now from farmer Jones as he was relied upon more. Farmer Jones was suffering badly from arthritis and Antonio was now his right hand around the farm.

Mary was able to live comfortably, purchasing more items for the cottage which was now restored to its former glory.

Nancy grew into a beautiful child with golden curls and blue eyes. She was her father's darling and he called her 'Angel baby'. She went with him sometimes to the farm where she was able to see the lambs and calves. Sadly the horse they had purchased died, but there were horses in farmer Jones' paddock.

Nancy attended the local village school and it was clear that she was a very bright child. Mary had already taught her to read and write so at the school she stood out as a star pupil.

When Nancy was ten years old Mary found herself pregnant again. This time she gave birth to twin boys who she called James and John. Nancy was able to help her mother and the boys flourished. They were a happy family until disaster struck. Antonio had been gathering wood when he tripped. He hit his head on a rock and gashed it badly. Mary had wondered why he was so long in coming home as his work had ended.

She went searching for him and found him unconscious and bleeding badly. She ran to farmer Jones who immediately got some help to carry him home. They put him to bed and sent for the doctor. It was hopeless, the wound was too deep, and Antonio slipped away. Farmer Jones paid for the funeral but Mary's grief was so deep she barely comprehended. She was totally devastated and inconsolable. She barely knew how to continue with her life and Nancy now had to care for her mother, the boys and still attend school.

Another tragedy occurred. Mrs Jones caught a fever and despite all the doctor's efforts she too passed away. Farmer Jones lost all interest in his farm. He sold his animals and became a shadow of the man he once was.

Farmer Jones could no longer help Mary although he knew she would suffer from the lack of his largesse. He really needed help now for himself as he too was struggling to stay afloat. This was when Mary had to beg for custom from neighbouring properties to do their washing.

The two boys and Nancy helped in the cottage and Nancy had progressed from being a pupil to teaching at the village school. The money from this, however, was very poor as the school was small. One of the teachers, Mrs Higgs, had taught Nancy pianoforte and allowed her to practise on her inherited piano.

CHAPTER 4

Time passed and Nancy was now eighteen and the boys were eight. They attended the village school where Nancy now taught. The boys tried to do their best in the little gardens and tried to keep growing the herbs and vegetables their father had planted. It became obvious that things were not going well. Sometimes Mary could not dry the washing for some customers, although others let her visit their house for her to do it on site. The boys gathered kindling for the oven and Mrs Higgs let Mary have some of her coal for the copper. It was obvious that they were struggling. One day Nancy spoke to her mother.

"Mother, I need to find work, so that I can get extra money for you and the boys."

"Not living in as a servant," gasped Mary.

"No! No! You taught me to read and write and the school also taught me so much. Mrs Higgs taught me to play the pianoforte, and as you know I am teaching at the school, but the money I get is so little, I am going to apply for a position as a governess. Yes, I will live in, but Mrs Higgs says that the money for such a position is good. I shall advertise in the national papers and also go to the nearest agency. In fact, as it is the end of the week at school, I will go tomorrow."

The next day Nancy put on her best navy gown and bonnet purchased some time ago from the local village shop. She walked to the nearest inn and caught the stagecoach to the nearest large town five miles away. This was where her grandparents lived, but she would not go there and beg. She believed that they had treated her mother most unfairly and knew that Antonio's parents lived in Italy.

She had planned the double action of placing an advertisement and also visiting an agency for some time before mentioning it to her mother. She had placed her advertisement and enquired about an agency. She was given the address by a kindly bespectacled gentleman, who also promised that her advertisement would be placed in the next edition. Nancy was able to pay for the advertisement and stagecoach from extra money that Mrs Higgs kindly gave to her.

Rowans Agency for the employment of young ladies was in Broadgate where the stagecoach stopped at the Leoftin Inn. She made her way there. Upon entering she now passed several pale-faced young girls sitting huddled together. They informed her that they were hoping to be employed as maid servants. A very superior lady descended upon her almost immediately, ignoring the young girls. She was obviously impressed with the way Nancy dressed and held herself.

"What position are you after, girl?" she enquired.

Nancy felt like rushing away but held her ground. "Governess," she replied.

"Oh! And what qualifications do you have?"

Nancy had come prepared with Mrs Higgs' testimonial. She held it out as she spoke.

"I can teach reading, writing and arithmetic. I have been doing this at the village school as my testimonial will confer. I can also teach history, geography, art, a little French and the pianoforte."

The supercilious woman looked impressed. She read Mrs Higgs' reference and looked up. "Well, Lord Derby has asked me to find a governess for his two daughters. They are six and seven years old. My fee is two guineas."

Nancy had foreseen this and handed over some of the money that Mrs Higgs had given to her.

"Here is the address. You may not suit of course. The address is in Kenilworth only a short distance from Coventry. The house is called Fairstow. A carrier is coming by shortly to take one girl for whom I have found a situation. He could drop you off. Wait here."

One girl Nancy had hitherto not seen, entered the room. She looked as if she had been weeping, but Nancy hesitated to ask the reason. The carrier came by with a horse and cart. The supercilious woman handed him his threepence and the girls climbed in to the cart.

There were only sacks upon which to sit, and Nancy was concerned for the state of her dress. Her companion sat down on the sacks, but turned her head away from Nancy. The road was fairly smooth, and the carrier dropped Nancy off at the turning in the road.

Climbing down she was rather bewildered as to which direction to take and had to ask directions from a passer-by. After only a short walk she could see an avenue which had gates at the entrance. There was a gatehouse with a surly occupant who confirmed the address and allowed her in when she stated the reason for her visit. As she walked along the drive, she felt dispirited. They had once been so happy as a family and now she had to pray that this position would be hers. She knew how badly Mary needed money and she wanted to repay her mother for the love and care she had received. If this all came to nothing, she would have wasted the two guineas and had barely enough to return home. There was of course hope from her advertisement, but that too may involve various costs.

CHAPTER 5

She now approached the large front door set back between two huge white pillars. She raised the heavy iron shaped knocker and let it fall. Immediately a man, whom she presumed was the butler, opened the door.

"Yes!" he said curtly. "I am Harrison, the butler."

"I have come about the position of governess," Nancy explained.

"His Lordship is at home, I will see if he is available. Wait here!"

Nancy was left on the large marble step. She was able to step back and look more carefully at the imposing building. Close to, it looked very large and she could see turrets, chimneys and many windows. She could see that the grounds were extensive. It was all so imposing Nancy could hardly comprehend it all.

The butler returned. "Follow me," he said.

Nancy was taken into a large hall, the floor of which was patterned with black and white tiles. Overhead was a huge chandelier.

"This way," the butler indicated. "What is your name, girl?" he asked.

"Nancy Ferran," she replied.

"Nancy Ferran," announced the butler as he opened the door to a room that led from a long corridor.

Nancy entered what she presumed was a library. Books lined the walls and at a mahogany desk sat a dark-haired man with dark bushy eyebrows. Nancy guessed that he was probably younger than he looked, possibly in his thirties.

"I was not expecting you!" he stated, but still rose as she entered the room.

"I am Lord Derby. Please be seated." He indicated to a velvet padded carved chair.

"I only went to the agency today," Nancy explained. "I was advised to come for an interview immediately."

"Hum!" the man muttered. "Well you are here now. May I see your references."

Nancy gave him Mrs Higgs' testimonial.

"This seems to be in order. You have obviously taught, but what training have you had with young children away from a school situation?"

"I have two brothers," explained Nancy. "And I help my mother with them. I love children and if my father had not died, would probably have stayed as a teacher at the village school."

Lord Derby did not enquire about her need for more lucrative employment. He obviously knew that village school teachers would earn very little and guessed that things must be difficult following the demise of her father.

"The salary is forty-five guineas a year," he stated. "That is above the average wage for a governess, but my girls need one at once. Their previous governess eloped with one of my footmen. When can you start?"

Nancy was rather overwhelmed. She had not really expected things to move so quickly.

"I have also advertised for a position," she confessed.

"How much did they charge?"

"One and sixpence."

Lord Derby opened a drawer and took out some money.

"Here is the one and sixpence. Now you can forget it. Don't bother with any replies that come in. I would like you to commence immediately. The housekeeper Mrs Chapman already has a room prepared, in fact it is the room of the last governess, but it has been cleaned and refurbished."

"I need to see my mother and gather my belongings," stuttered Nancy.

"I could have sent servants for that," stated Lord Derby. "But, however, I will do as you wish. Where do you live?"

"Merridon," said Nancy.

Lord Derby rang a bell and a footman entered.

"Tell Charles to prepare the carriage and horses to go to Merridon at once. This young lady will be travelling."

"Certainly, my Lord," the footman bowed out.

"My coachman will take you home today. He will collect you at seven in the morning. You will of course be on approval for one month. My girls are with my sister at present, one mile from here. They will be returning later in the day. You will of course see them tomorrow.

"Here is three guineas in advance of your wages. I believe the agency fee is two guineas, here is five guineas in total."

Lord Derby escorted Nancy to the door and she was immediately ushered out by the butler. The carriage was at the door. The coachman, Charles, was silent and she had to climb into the carriage by herself.

The coach was luxurious with red velvet padded seating. Nancy just felt confused, however, and felt as if she was in a dream.

At last they were in Merridon and Charles had to ask directions to the cottage. He stopped outside and Nancy climbed out.

"I am going to the nearest Inn to rest and water the horses," he explained. "I shall be back in the morning at seven o'clock."

CHAPTER 6

Nancy walked into the house and Mary hugged her. The twins gathered round. They had all seen the coach and they were wondering what had happened. Mary made Nancy some tea and they sat round the table patiently waiting for an explanation. Nancy told them what had happened and that Lord Derby wished her to commence her duties at once. Nancy gave Mary the extra three guineas that had been given to her by Lord Derby and Mary took it gratefully, but when she heard that Nancy was actually leaving at seven o'clock, she wept. This caused the twins to cry also. Nancy had to ask her mother to explain to Mrs Higgs that she had immediate employment as a governess and wrote a note deeply thanking her for all her kindness.

Nancy went to gather up her few belongings but with tears streaming down her face too. There was one fewer mouth to feed now, and the three guineas would last her mother for some time, but she wondered if she was paid monthly, how she could get the money home. She hoped she could find an honest carrier. She would also need to return home herself and wondered if Charles would once more be available.

So many questions, with no obvious answers and she began to sob. Mary came into the room.

"Don't cry, child," she said. "You have done what you believe to be right. God will be with you and guide you."

"I am only on trial," confessed Nancy. "I may not suit. I haven't even seen the children yet. They may not take to me, I also have the impression that there is no Lady Derby. I have been given no information and everything seems to be so rushed."

"Don't worry, child," comforted Mary. "I am sure that all will be revealed in time. If you are unhappy, however, you know that we shall be happy for you to return. As they say, as one door closes another one opens. You know that our love will go with you."

Nancy slept soundly during the night as she felt totally exhausted.

She arose and dressed at six. Mary was also up and about. The twins were still sleeping and Nancy decided it was better not to say goodbye as it was all too painful and better for the boys for her just to be gone. She had tea and bread and butter, then brought down her few possessions in the carpet bag and a sack bag that she had.

Charles arrived promptly at seven o'clock and there was hardly any time for Nancy to hug her mother as Charles loaded the bags and also indicated for her to climb in promptly. This may have been as well because Mary and Nancy felt choked with emotion.

As Nancy climbed into the carriage, she gave a final wave to her mother and they set off. Nancy to her new life.

CHAPTER 7

They soon seemed to be in Kenilworth and at the gatehouse to Fairstow. As they drove along the long drive, Lord Derby's house appeared into view. In the early morning sun the windows gleamed and the turrets looked even more imposing. She glanced at the grounds and could see a lake glistening in the distance. There were statues in the grounds surrounded by roses and topiary. There were also several other buildings that could be summer houses.

Charles stopped the carriage at the entrance to the house and this time the butler opened the door. A doorman came out and took her bags and another servant came out and escorted her inside. Mrs Chapman, the housekeeper, appeared and said rather curtly, "I will show you to your room."

Nancy meekly followed Mrs Chapman through the large hall and up two flights of stairs. The main staircase led from the hall and was wide and elaborate. The second staircase was more narrow and led to a landing along which were several doors.

"This room is the nursery and school room," Mrs Chapman informed her. She just threw open the door and Nancy could see shelves with books and toys, but also chairs and desks. Mrs Chapman quickly closed the door and led Nancy to another door some way down the corridor.

"This is your room," she stated. "Mason the footman will bring your bags, although there doesn't seem to be very much."

Nancy felt that Mrs Chapman was being a little sarcastic, but just thanked her quietly.

"The girls are with his Lordship at the moment," volunteered the housekeeper.

"Anyway, this is your room. I will come to fetch you to see his Lordship and the girls in half an hour."

Mrs Chapman turned on her heels and with a rustle of bombazine, left.

Nancy entered the room. She had a nice surprise. A window opened onto the grounds at the rear, and she could just see the glistening of the lake in the distance. There was a canopied bed, wardrobe, dressing table, desk and chair, a settee, washstand with jug and basin, pale blue curtains at the window and a pale blue patterned carpet on the floor. The room was a reasonable size and Nancy felt immediately at home in this cosy room. The furniture was dark oak and obviously expensive. The room was far better than the one Nancy had firstly shared with her brothers and latterly with her mother.

She took off her cloak and bonnet and put these in the wardrobe. There was water in the water jug, together with a soft towel, so she washed her face and hands. She still wore the navy dress originally purchased from the second-hand shop. Mrs Higgs had given her the dark blue cloak that had previously been owned by the deceased sister. She did have two grey gowns that she had worn when teaching at the village school. These too she unpacked and hung them in the wardrobe. This had a bottom drawer into which she placed her sparse underwear. Her shoes were the serviceable ones she had purchased for school.

Looking into the mirror on the dressing table, she smoothed her hair just in time for Mrs Chapman to open the door and state, "His Lordship is waiting for you now in the library."

She seemed to glare at Nancy as she spoke, but Nancy just quietly said, "Thank you," and followed Mrs Chapman down the two flights of stairs, once again along the corridor, leading from the hall into the room that Nancy had previously guessed to be the library. There was a cheery fire sparkling in the fireplace and two small girls were sitting on stools beside it. Lord Derby rose from behind his mahogany desk, held out his hand and smiled.

"Welcome," he said. "May I introduce my nieces, Emily, who is seven years of age and Anne who is six.

Both children rose but looked shy and confused.

"This is Nancy Ferran, who is to be your new governess," Lord Derby stated.

"I am very pleased to be here," said Nancy, smiling. She walked up to both girls and gave them a hug.

"I have twin brothers who are eight years of age. I love them dearly, but it will be lovely to be a governess to two such pretty young girls."

The children smiled shyly.

"Let us all be seated," he said. The children sat back on their padded stools and Lord Derby once again indicated for Nancy to sit on the carved padded chair upon which she had previously sat for her interview. Lord Derby volunteered the information: "My younger brother and his wife visited India three years ago, leaving the children with my sister. Unfortunately, they caught cholera and passed away. My sister, Cassandra, already has three children and in his will, my brother left the children to my care. I was surprised as I am unmarried but I was devoted to my brother and his wife and of course follow his wishes."

Nancy cast a glance at the children as he spoke. They just looked into the fire as if Lord Derby had not spoken.

She thought to herself, "What can they do? What can they say? They were so young when they lost their parents, but what about their original home?"

Nancy dared to speak. "What happened to their family home?"

"It is leased at present," Lord Derby replied. "The money from this is being put into a bank account for the children's future. I shall not sell the property, although I am the executor of my brother's will, until they are old enough to understand. If it is ever sold the money will go to them equally. There are also things in their home they may wish to keep."

Nancy could see the reasoning behind all this and Lord Derby went up in her estimation.

"Well, shall I take the children now to the school room?" she queried.

"Certainly, and thank you. I will leave the children in what I am sure are your capable hands. If there is anything that you need, please ask Mrs Chapman, who will inform me, or give a note to Mason, the footman. Please feel free to have anything that will enhance their education. Also make good use of the library."

"Thank you," replied Nancy. "It will take me a few days to ascertain what we shall need. I saw that the school room was well stocked with books, and I presume that there are writing materials there. However, I did not notice a piano. They are a little young to learn, but I can teach the pianoforte as you have seen in my testimonial."

"Oh goodness," laughed Lord Derby. "We have several pianos. We have a music room, with a grand and an upright. There are pianos in the sitting rooms, main hall and the ballroom."

Nancy was rather overwhelmed with this, but secretly thought that the music room seemed to be the best room for the children when the time was right.

Nancy decided that it was time to depart. "Come, children," said Nancy. "Let us commence our day."

Mason seemed to appear by magic and they exited the library.

Mrs Chapman appeared again. "The children have all meals served in the nursery," she volunteered. "No doubt you will wish to eat with them. Breakfast is at eight o'clock, usually lunch at twelve, afternoon tea is served at three and the children's evening meal at five o'clock. The children usually go to bed at seven o'clock."

Nancy noted down all this information in her head. She knew that a governess was higher than a servant, but not a true member of the family. Apparently she was too menial to eat with Lord Derby or his friends. She knew that kitchen staff, including the butler, housekeeper, maids and footmen ate in the kitchen. She wondered if Lord Derby had a good cook, but presumed that he did. She knew that at least she would have regular food and felt grateful for her lovely bedroom.

CHAPTER 8

They all went up the staircases to the combined nursery and school room. It soon became apparent that the girls could already read and write but not in cursive writing. Nancy decided that this was the first thing that she would teach them.

There were plenty of writing books and pencils in the school room together with chalks and a blackboard. Nancy began to show the children how to make simple words such as an, at, do, etc. They were willing pupils and it was soon time for lunch. A young maid, Fanny, delivered a light lunch which they all ate at the nursery table and another maid, Agnes, cleared away. The servants just gave Nancy a brief smile, but made no conversation. In the afternoon Nancy decided to take the children into the grounds to explain some of the flowers and she soon found a herb garden with which she was very familiar. The children enjoyed picking and smelling some of the herbs and Nancy simplified their usage as much as possible.

They returned for afternoon tea and then Nancy read them a story from Hans Andersen. It was soon time for the evening meal and then miraculously some matronly soul who said she was now the children's nurse/nanny appeared.

She said her name was Mrs Compton and her position was to wash the children, get them dressed in the morning and also to put them to bed.

Nancy had not seen the children's bedroom, but apparently at this young age they shared a room with twin beds. Their room was bright with windows again looking out onto the main grounds. It had yellow silk walls, gold curtains and furniture covered in yellow velvet or satin. The main bedcover was yellow and the carpet gold.

There were white shelves along one wall on which there were perched toy animals and dolls aplenty. There were board games and in one corner of the room a huge rocking horse.

Nancy could see that the children were well cared for and had all that they needed.

Despite Mrs Compton's administrations, the children begged Nancy to stay and read them a story; they did not appear to like Mrs Compton. Nancy herself was feeling tired and a little homesick but of course agreed to do so. She found the book 'Alice in Wonderland' by Lewis Carroll and enchanted the children with the tale of the white rabbit, and some of Alice's adventures underground. When she could see both children were sleepy she gave them a goodnight kiss and returned to her room.

The bed was turned down, a night light burning, there was warm water in the water jug. As it was late summer, the evenings were getting cooler and there was even a small fire burning in the fireplace. Nancy was very impressed with this care, but noticed that there were no books in the bedroom, apart from a Bible in a drawer in the dressing table.

Nancy knew now for certain that there was a library but wondered if she would be allowed to borrow a book. She re-opened the bedroom door and the young footman appeared.

"Do you think I may borrow a book from the library?" she questioned.

"I do not know, ma'am," he replied. "I will go and ask his Lordship."

"No! No!" worried Nancy. "I cannot let him be disturbed."

"Do not concern yourself, ma'am," the young footman replied and hurried off.

Nancy felt dreadful. She returned into her room and sat in the window seat. She had only been at the mansion, because that's what it was, for such a short time, and she was probably taking or thinking of taking liberties to which she was not entitled. Suddenly there was a knock at the door. She rose and opened it. The young footman stood there. He had three books in his hand.

"His Lordship has sent three books by Dickens that you may have read, but found interesting. 'The Old Curiosity Shop', 'Nicholas Nickleby' and 'Great Expectations'. His Lordship is entertaining a friend in the library, but said that when the library is free you are most welcome to enter and to choose any books that yourself or the children may require."

Nancy blushed with embarrassment. Whatever had come over her to be so presumptuous. She appreciated Lord Derby's kindness. She thanked the young footman and chose Nicholas Nickleby, then returned into her room. She sat in the chair and opened 'Nicholas Nickleby'. She had read it before but always found the story fascinating. As the outside light faded, as did the night light, so Nancy prepared herself for bed, and soon fell asleep in the bed with the feathery mattress and downy pillows. She had never before experienced such luxury and despite missing her mother and brothers, felt very fortunate to be in such a comfortable home.

CHAPTER 9

Nancy awoke early as she had at home. She could already hear the sounds of activity at Fairstow. She realised that some of the servants would rise at five o'clock in the morning and knew that their day would be long. She thought of her mother struggling with the laundry and she felt guilty curled up on a soft feather bed. She rose and looked out of the bedroom window. Already there were gardeners in the grounds.

She remembered Charles who had driven the carriage and realised that there must be stables somewhere in the grounds. She guessed that Charles and other grooms probably had rooms above the stables. Nancy realised that there was still so much to take in and that she was of course in a completely different world.

She had heard from her mother about the disagreement with her grandfather, and Mary had sometimes referred to her previous life, which had obviously been quite different than the one into which she, Nancy, had been born. Mary had never said too much, however, and had always been very much in love with her father Antonio. Nancy pondered that it must have been very hard for her mother to leave a life of what sounded like comparative luxury, to go to the cottage and on many occasions struggle. As Nancy mused, a knock came to her bedroom door. She called, 'Enter'.

A young maid entered. She could only have been about twelve. Again this gave Nancy food for thought.

"I have brought your hot water, miss," she mumbled, "and Mrs Chapman says that breakfast will be soon served in the nursery. The children's nanny has dressed the children."

Nancy remembered that breakfast was at eight and hastily washed and dressed. In the soft feather bed she had indulged in day dreaming, once again remembering her mother and her father. She had never seemed to have much time previously to contemplate about her mother's previous life, but now in these new surroundings it had brought home to her once again, what an enormous change had happened to her mother's life. For the first time it entered her mind that much as she missed her mother and brothers, how would she cope now after only briefly experiencing this present luxury, if she returned to the rather basic necessitates of the cottage. This made her feel ashamed at such a thought and she hastened to the school room.

CHAPTER 10

Porridge, bread, butter and cheese, plus tea was laid out on the table in the nursery. There was also an assortment of fruit. The children were already seated and Nancy greeted them fondly. They were indeed lovely children. Both had blond curls and blue eyes and despite Emily being a little taller, they could almost have been mistaken for twins.

They all settled down to the breakfast and the new day at Fairstow commenced. They spent the morning again learning cursive writing and after lunch doing some basic arithmetic. The girls were bright and it was easy to teach them together.

After afternoon tea they again walked in the garden and Nancy picked a rose for them to copy on their drawing pads. They returned, putting the rose in water and soon Fanny appeared with the evening meal. There was soup, fish and potatoes followed by baked apples and custard. Tea was again served as the drink, but water was also available.

To Nancy's surprise Mason appeared at the nursery door.

"Lord Derby would like to see you all in the library," he said. "There is plenty of time as the main meal is not served until seven o'clock."

Nancy was a little worried at this, wondering if anything had gone wrong, but as soon as Agnes removed the remains of the meal away, she ushered the children downstairs to the library. She was now able to find this easily.

Once again, Lord Derby was at his mahogany desk and bade them to be seated as before.

"How are you coping with my nieces?" he enquired to Nancy.

"Very well, my Lord," replied Nancy. "They are very intelligent children and I feel fortunate to be their governess."

"A good answer," smiled Lord Derby. "Well, children, what do you think of your new governess?" he enquired of the children.

Nancy thought this a rather impertinent question to ask, whilst she was in the room.

The children obviously thought this too, and both hesitated before responding.

Emily answered: "We are happy."

Anna also joined in: "Miss read to us before we went to sleep."

Nancy spoke hastily, "Girls, please call me Nancy. This would make you feel much more comfortable."

Lord Derby laughed. "Well, we will all agree Nancy it is and Nancy it will be. I had the feeling that things were going well. In fact, at the end of the week I have guests arriving. I should be pleased if you would come down after your evening meal to be introduced to them."

Emily dared to enquire, "Who is coming, Uncle?"

"Oh, some friends and their families from neighbouring estates. I have lost touch with my neighbours, following my brother's demise and wish to re-establish relationships, but have recently been too busy to entertain, after recent events. My sister and her husband are unfortunately in Scotland at present."

Nancy realised that Lord Derby must be talking about closing down his brother's and sister-in-law's affairs, but remained silent.

"I shall therefore expect you in the salon next Saturday at six-thirty. We are delaying dinner until eight-thirty this weekend. It will only take half an hour and Emily and Anna you will only be delayed from your bedtime for a short while. Are you agreeable to this?" Lord Derby turned to Nancy.

"Of course, my Lord. Too many people may be a little confusing for the children, but I am sure all will be well."

"Am I being reprimanded?" queried Lord Derby. "I just feel it was time for my guests to really meet my new family and of course," (he added shyly), "their new governess."

Nancy blushed at this and the children nudged each other, smiling.

They returned to their rooms. The nurse, Mrs Compton, took charge of the children completely that evening and Nancy retreated to her room. She wondered what she would wear on the Saturday. It would have to be her best navy dress, as she only had her old school teaching clothes. She knew that the girls had lovely dresses hanging in the armoire in their bedrooms so there was no problem there. She continued to read 'Nicholas Nickleby' but wondered if she dared now to return to the library to find a book of her choice. She crept out of her room and down the staircase. She could hear the kitchen staff preparing for the full evening meal in the dining room and guessed that now Lord Derby's valet was putting the finishing touches to his dinner suit.

She soon found the library again and set down 'Nicholas Nickleby' on a side table. She could smell the remains of Lord Derby's cigar that he obviously smoked in there. There were so many books all beautifully bound and a small step ladder set aside to reach the top shelves. She thought that she would settle for the life of Marie Antoinette and was searching the history section of the library when the door opened. She was poised on the small step ladder searching through the books, but the scents made her take an involuntary step back. She could feel herself falling, but suddenly two strong arms held her as she fell.

"I thought I heard a noise as I was passing," said Lord Derby. "And I was right." Nancy was crushed against his chest as he gently set her down on her feet.

"You did indicate that I could borrow books for myself and the girls," stuttered Nancy as she extracted herself from Lord Derby's arms.

For a moment he seemed to hold her, and she felt her head swim. Lord Derby took a step backwards and dropped his arms.

"You could have had a nasty fall," he volunteered. "Did you find the book for which you were looking?"

"No!" admitted Nancy. "But I found one on the life of Louis XIV and that will be exciting to read."

"I am so glad that you found a suitable book," stated Lord Derby. He looked at Nancy carefully. She still had the golden curls of childhood and had developed into a very beautiful girl. She could almost be the older sister to his nieces, mused Lord Derby.

"I must go to dinner, do stay if you wish."

"No, no, I have my book. Thank you so much," Nancy managed to say and turned to the door.

Although Mason was outside, Lord Derby held the door open for her.

"I am so glad that you are here," he uttered.

Nancy exited along the corridor to the staircase.

"What made him say that when I have been here for such a very short time," she pondered.

Although eighteen, she had never had time to really consider her appearance. It had always been almost a battle for survival, either trying to make her mark in the village school, or helping with the twins, and particularly difficult after her father died. She had let her hair grow long, but had swept it back for her teaching and now as a governess. In the fracas in the library it had come loose and had been cascading down her back as Lord Derby had caught her.

She had no idea that Lord Derby had suddenly realised that he had a very beautiful girl in his arms, but she sensed that he was certainly not displeased with her.

Nancy read until the night light went out and drank the carafe of water that was always placed upon her bed table, at night, together with some wafer biscuits to eat.

She climbed again into the luxurious bed and despite wanting to go over the events of the day, was soon asleep.

CHAPTER 11

Saturday came, it was an unusual day. Carriages arrived with guests and the butler, housekeeper, servants and footman were all at full stretch to take the guests to their rooms.

Nancy decided to take the children into the grounds away from all the excitement. She decided to take them to the lake as it was some distance from all the melee around the house.

It beckoned gleaming from the sun, and Nancy and the children walked leisurely towards it. There were trees growing around it and some branches overhanging the lake. Some ducks could be seen swimming in the distance and Nancy felt assured that her decision to bring the children here was an excellent one. Some tall reeds and rushes bordered parts of the lake and small ripples in the water indicated that there may well be fish beneath the surface. Nancy thought that the lesson could be about cold-blooded vertebrates, and how they survived in water. There was a lovely stone carved seat at one point by the side of the lake, upon which they all sat. At first Nancy let the children just enjoy sitting by the waterside and she too felt much enjoyment from just looking at the water. It did in fact have movement because in the distance they could hear a waterfall. Nancy guessed this cascaded into a stream which probably passed through several estates, ending in the River Avon, which was the main river at Stratford.

Just as Nancy was about to commence her lesson, there was a wild, "Halloo," and a young boy of about fourteen came crashing towards them. He had no adult with him at all. Nancy spoke.

"Hello, dear sir. Should you not be with your mama and papa?"

"No, I should not," retorted the boy rudely. "Mama would not let me go away to school, although that is what Papa wanted and I have to have a tutor. I have managed to escape from him as Mama insisted that he accompanied us here. I just want some freedom from them all. Anyway, who are you?"

"I am the governess, Nancy Ferran," replied Nancy. "And this is Emily and this is Anna, the nieces of Lord Derby."

The children only smiled an acknowledgement.

"Oh. Well I am Thomas Burstow. We live in the estate next to Lord Derby. Mama hopes he will marry Isobelle, my eldest sister. She is eighteen and here as well. I am tired of hearing about it all, it is so boring. Do you know how to make stones jump across water?" he suddenly added.

The girls just shook their heads.

"I do think you should return to your family," repeated Nancy. "I think that perhaps we should walk back with you."

"Stuff and nonsense," retorted the boy. "I'm not a baby to be led around."

So saying, he then picked up a round stone from the edge of the lake and sent it skimming across the water.

"Oh! Poor show." It only went in with one plop. "I can make stones do at least four jumps in the air."

So saying, he picked up more round stones and moved closer to the edge of the lake.

"I need to be closer," Thomas stated. "I am very proud of my prowess at stone throwing."

Nancy became alarmed at his proximity to the water's edge.

"Do be careful," she urged. "The bank may be slippery."

"You sound like my mama. She hardly lets me have any fun. I was allowed to stay with Rupert my friend when he came home from Stowe. They have a lake also and he taught me this trick. You'll see in a minute how clever it is."

Thomas swung round, to angle his shot, but in so doing, caught his foot in one of the reeds edging the lake. He completely lost his balance and fell forward into the lake. He did not appear to move, and without hesitation Nancy said to the girls, "Run quickly for help."

Obediently they began to run back to the house, but fortunately two gardeners were still working close by. The girls rushed to them first, explained what had happened and then carried on to the house to tell the boy's mother. The gardeners had been too busy to notice the events.

Nancy meantime did not hesitate. She threw off her shoes and waded into the water. Fortunately, there was a tree branch nearby to which she clung. She could not swim, but hung on to the branch with one hand, whilst clutching the boy's collar, who was luckily near to the tree, to hold his head above water. The gardeners came rapidly, and pulled the boy onto the bank. He had a small bruise on his head and had obviously bumped his head as he fell. He was breathing and conscious but looked very pale. The gardeners loosened his clothing and one of them, being strong, prepared to lift the boy in his arms to take him back to the house. Nancy, now out of the water, cold and dripping, picked up her shoes and put them on. Her feet were frozen and her best navy dress now completely sodden from the waist down. She followed the trio back to the house but as the gardeners neared the door, the second gardener at the ready in case the burden was too great, the boy's mama came flying out of the door. She was crying and screaming, having already heard via the girls what had occurred. The girls had gone into the house and of course firstly told the butler, who had already alerted two footmen to go to the boy's aid. Mrs Chapman, the housekeeper, had told two maids to prepare a hot bath and of course she told the boy's father.

The footman took the boy from the gardeners and putting him on an armed chair hastily carried him upstairs. The tub followed and hot water in pails and towels followed, carried by servants.

No grateful words were given to the gardeners who turned away, maybe to their own cottages, particularly the one who had carried the boy from the lake. They seemed to have expected no acknowledgement and turned away automatically when other help appeared.

Nancy, however, stood dripping on the doorstep. Mrs Burstow saw her.

"I believe you are the cause of all this trouble," she shrieked. "I have heard that you are the governess and took the girls down to the lake. A stupid thing to do and it probably tempted my poor Thomas to follow. If he is really ill after this, I shall blame you. You are not fit to be a governess, obviously far too young and inexperienced."

Nancy just stood trembling. Perhaps what Mrs Burstow said was partially true, but she had gone into the lake and probably saved the impetuous boy from drowning.

Lord Derby suddenly appeared.

"Mrs Burstow," he said. "I suggest you go upstairs and comfort your son. He is having every care and attention and of course I have sent for Doctor Morley. In fact, here he is now."

Doctor Morley had been fetched by Charles and hastily stepped from the carriage where he was ushered into the house by the butler.

"It is all the fault of this girl," continued Mrs Burstow. "Thomas would not have thought of going to the lake."

Lord Derby intervened. "I believe your son went to the lake some time after the governess and the children, but that is not the point now. Doctor Morley will check him over and

...," he paused, looking at Nancy. "I suggest Miss Ferran goes to her room and I will send a servant to attend her."

He grabbed Nancy's elbow and ushered her inside.

"Mrs Chapman," he said, addressing the housekeeper. "Please see that Miss Ferran is attended to at once."

Nancy squelched up the stairs followed by a reluctant Mrs Chapman. There was a servant by her door, but no hot tub. She was helped out of her dripping dress and the servant, who introduced herself as Gladys, promised to get the clothes and petticoat washed and ironed. Nancy took off her shoes and stockings and sank onto the bed. She remembered the children and with the help of Gladys, hastily got dressed in one of her grey gowns, washed her hands and face, thanked Gladys and went quickly to the school room.

The children were just sitting as if waiting for her.

"Oh Miss," uttered Emily. "That boy was so stupid and would have drowned but for you."

Anna threw her arms around Nancy. The school room door opened and Mrs Chapman entered.

"I will have hot drinks brought up," she stated. She looked at Nancy rather frostily. "Doctor Morley says that Thomas is quite well apart from a slight bruise. A rest in bed today will see him perfectly well."

Nancy drew a breath of relief. It was apparent that Thomas was hopelessly spoiled. His mother had no idea that he had already played by a lake with his friend Rupert, but she realised that any words at this time would be wasted.

CHAPTER 12

o her amazement, the school room door suddenly opened again and Lord Derby appeared.

"One of the under gardeners saw exactly what happened," he informed her. "He was too far away from immediate help, but he saw you arrive at the lake with the girls and Thomas came some time afterwards. I also hear that you went into the lake, and probably saved the boy from drowning."

"I cannot swim," confessed Nancy, "but I was able to hang onto a branch to rescue him. At least to keep his head above water."

"Well done, my girl," smiled Lord Derby. "And how do you feel?"

"I am well, my Lord, thank you. I am just sorry that all this has occurred at the commencement of your weekend with the guests."

Lord Derby sighed. "I wish of course that I had not proposed it. I had no idea that Mrs Burstow would bring her son. I thought him too young and that he would stay at home with his tutor. I knew of course that Isobelle Burstow would be coming."

Nancy said nothing again. She had not met Isobelle Burstow and in fact had met only Mrs Burstow. She remembered that she and the girls were originally to be introduced to all the guests before seven o'clock. She didn't know how to approach this point.

"I shall still expect yourself and the girls at six-thirty," he uttered.

Nancy had to speak.

"The girls will be suitably attired," she offered. "But I think that I should not be with them. My navy blue gown is my best and that is now being washed and ironed, but may not be ready by this evening."

Lord Derby frowned. "It is Saturday and shops are open. The girls can be looked after by Mrs Compton. The carriage has just returned from taking Doctor Morley home. It is still outside. My guests are all still settling into their rooms and lunch is being sent to each room. Croquet is arranged by a Master of Ceremonies I have hired for the afternoon. Come!"

He beckoned to Nancy to follow him. Confused, this she did. Lord Derby ushered her downstairs to the amazement of Mason and Mrs Compton, also the butler, and helped her into the carriage. He sat silently beside her until they reached some shops. One had lovely gowns and bonnets in the window. Lord Derby spoke, "Go inside, pick a gown and tell them to put it onto my account. I shall remain in the carriage."

Nancy tentatively opened the door and was met by a large well dressed lady. She had obviously seen the carriage outside and was beaming. "What may I do for you?" she asked.

Nancy spoke at once." I am governess to Lord Derby's girls. There has been an accident and I require a serviceable suitable gown for my position."

The proprietress nodded. "I have just the one that I know will fit. It was a for a lady's maid but in the end not required. It is in royal blue, and without too many trimmings." She sent a girl to rapidly produce the gown. She led Nancy to a room where it was tried on. It fitted perfectly.

"May I keep it on?" Nancy urged.

"Certainly. I see the carriage is waiting outside. I will parcel up your grey gown. Lord Derby has an account here for senior servants and the housekeeper. I hope you enjoy the gown, my dear."

Nancy picked up the parcel of her old gown and exited the shop.

"That was very rapid," exclaimed Lord Derby. "But you look delightful."

In next to no time they were back at Fairstow. By now some guests were playing croquet and Lord Derby smiled at Nancy.

"I will join my guests," he stated. "I am sure that there will be some lunch left for you in the school room. Try not to worry as I am sure that Thomas will be fine and thank you again for all that you did."

Lord Derby left for the garden. Nancy wondered if he had had any lunch. She went into the house and up the stairs. The girls had had lunch and were playing with their dolls.

"You look lovely," exclaimed Emily. "Is that a new dress?"

"Your uncle kindly let me have this as a replacement," said Nancy, keeping the matter simple.

"There is some lunch over here for you under the cloth," explained Anna.

Nancy did not feel hungry, but ate a little bread and cheese and drank some milk that was left. Mrs Compton had obviously gone down to the kitchen and left the girls to their own devices.

"What shall we do this afternoon?" enquired Emily.

"I will read some more of 'Alice in Wonderland'," offered Nancy and this she did.

Teatime came and went and they could hear the laughter from guests in the garden.

CHAPTER 13

It was soon time for the girls to be dressed to appear in the salon at Lord Derby's request. They chose their own gowns from the armoire and Mrs Compton came into their bedroom to help.

Nancy retreated to her room and of course had little to do as she was already wearing the blue gown.

To her amazement, the navy dress was on the bed, looking quite perfect. Nancy decided to put this back on and folded the new dress and placed this in the wardrobe.

She again washed in the water kindly placed in the room and re-combed her hair. Her shoes were still rather damp, but she could do nothing about this.

At six-fifteen, she went to fetch the girls who looked quite lovely. Anna had on a frilly yellow gown and Emily a muslin layered pink gown. The girls had matching ribbons in their hair and lovely satin shoes.

"You look lovely, girls," ventured Nancy.

"You are not wearing your new dress," exclaimed Emily.

"I am your governess," smiled Nancy. "The guests will wish to see you."

All the guests were seated in the salon when Harrison the butler showed them into the room. Lord Derby, looking very handsome in evening wear, rose and took the girls by their hands.

"May I introduce Emily and Anna, my nieces," he explained.

One woman cooed, "Oh what lovely children, they are so pretty."

Mrs Burstow and her husband were in the salon.

"That is the dreadful girl with them who caused my son's accident," Mrs Burstow said loudly. "It is only by chance he didn't die. He is now recovering from his ordeal in his bedroom after a visit from Doctor Morley. I don't know how that girl can show her face here," she added.

All the guests gasped and looked at Nancy with contempt.

Lord Derby intervened. "Nancy probably saved the boy's life," he uttered. "One of the under gardeners saw the whole event even though some distance away. I think the boy was too near to the edge of the lake and slipped. My governess does not swim, but she went into the lake hanging onto a branch and kept the boy's head above water until my nieces fetched immediate help."

Mrs Burstow did not give in. "If the governess had not taken your nieces to the lake, my boy would not have gone anywhere near the place."

"Apparently your son came a little after my governess and the girls. We cannot blame anyone. It was just a dreadful accident."

"Dreadful is the word," retorted Mrs Burstow, but as she was hoping for a liaison between her daughter Isobelle and Lord Derby, she decided to behave a little more friendly. "Well luckily my boy is recovering well."

Harrison, the butler, entered. "Dinner is served in the dining room," he announced. The gentlemen took their ladies by the arm and Lord Derby took Isobelle Burstow on his arm. However, he turned to Nancy and said, "Thank you for bringing the girls. I do hope that you suffer no ill effects from your bravery and thank you again for all that you did."

Lord Derby made no comment on the fact that Nancy was not wearing the new blue gown that had been purchased.

She turned and left the salon, followed by Emily and Anna.

Emily spoke as they ascended the stairs. "I am so glad that Uncle realised how you helped that boy."

Nancy replied, "Well, let us hope he really is well tomorrow. It could all have been so much worse. But look, here is Mrs Compton to help you to bed."

As she spoke, Mrs Compton appeared and swept the girls to their bedroom. She gave Nancy a hard look, as if she too really believed that somehow Nancy was to blame for all the upset, and ushered the girls away, but Nancy noticed that she pushed them.

Fortunately, some kind soul had left a covered dish of food in her room together with a glass of milk. Nancy was not really hungry, but ate what was prepared. She felt drained and exhausted. She lay down on the bed in her clothes and soon fell asleep.

Nancy suddenly awoke. The house seemed quiet and yet all her senses were alert. She had read the book on Louis XIV. She had in fact read it before but always found it an interesting fact of French history. The night light had not been lit but there were matches there to do so. She wondered if she could go down to the library and find another book. It would at least give her something to do, even if she did not read it until the morning. She felt unsettled and also was still wondering how Thomas was faring.

There were lighters on the stairs, and once again Nancy crept to the library. Mason was on duty, but he just nodded at Nancy.

She entered the library and to her amazement Lord Derby was there reclining in a sofa chair. She immediately made as if to withdraw, but Lord Derby rose.

"How lovely to see you. Please don't leave. Perhaps we can have a little chat before you finally retire."

Nancy blushed. "I am returning the book on Louis XIV and thought to choose another," she stuttered.

"Of course you may choose a book, but please sit down. I am in the mood to talk after today."

Nancy sat down obediently. Lord Derby had changed from his evening attire into a smoking jacket, but he put out his cigar. He looked at Nancy. She was still in her own navy dress, but her hair had come undone and was curling down her back. One ringlet fell over her shoulder. Lord Derby swallowed. "She really is a lovely girl," he thought. He had been nudged towards Isobelle Burstow all evening. Not only had she been seated next to him at dinner, but Mrs Burstow had edged her towards him at every opportunity. Isobelle Burstow was a pretty girl, nut brown curls and beautifully gowned, but she was very limited in her conversation and did not appeal to him at all. He realised the hopes of Mr and Mrs Burstow, but sadly for them, he did not see Isobelle as his wife.

CHAPTER 14

For a while Lord Derby said nothing and they just sat in companiable silence, then Lord Derby spoke.

"This has not been a good start to the weekend on many counts. The croquet did not really go as well as I hoped, as some of the men appeared to be angry if they miss hit the ball and it did not go through the hoops. They all appeared to miss the peg. The evening meal was good of course, but the musical concert I arranged did not suit some of the ladies."

Nancy noticed that he did not include the fracas that Mrs Burstow created over Thomas.

"How is Thomas now?" she enquired.

"Very well, the bruise has already completely gone due to a cold compress and he is up and about in his room complaining because he did not attend the evening meal."

Nancy smiled wryly. "I wonder what he will do tomorrow."

"I think his father is taking him home in their carriage, which will return on Monday to take home his wife and daughter. I think that is a wise decision.

"Tomorrow after lunch I had arranged a picnic by the lake, but in the circumstances do not now think that a good idea. I shall rearrange the picnic nearer to the woods that edge my estate. I do regret this weekend. As I said, I had lost touch with many of my neighbours but time changes people. I wish my sister and her husband, Lord Fanshaw, had been present. I should have approached it more gradually and just waited for my sister and her husband and maybe invited Lord and Lady Horton and Lord and Lady Clements whom I know very well."

Nancy remained silent.

"I shouldn't throw all of this at you, my dear, but I just needed to unburden myself."

"I appreciate your confidence, my Lord," she said.

"You are a very lovely girl," Lord Derby suddenly uttered.

Nancy blushed.

"Why did you not wear the new gown that was purchased?"

"The navy one was kindly washed, ironed and returned. I felt it more appropriate to wear as a governess."

"The new gown suited you well. Remember that my nieces obviously care for you already, and that makes you a part of the family. Is your room comfortable?"

"Oh yes. It is delightful with the most lovely view of the rear grounds."

"Good. Remember to ask the servants to provide you with anything you need. I will ensure a maid is always available to you. Just ring the bell. I will give instructions to this effect. Do you require anything more for the school room?"

"No, my Lord, not at present."

"Then I will leave you to choose your book."

Lord Derby walked past and gave Nancy's shoulder a squeeze.

"Remember that my nieces are very important to me."

"As I have said previously, I am very fond of them already. I feel very privileged to be here."

"We are the ones privileged. Goodnight, my dear."

Lord Derby exited from the room and left Nancy pondering on his kindness. She hastily chose another book, not using the steps this time, an encyclopaedia that would be informative to her and useful in teaching the children. Mason was still outside. He said "Goodnight" and she climbed the stairs to her bedroom.

As she undressed – it was too late to summon a maid if one was available for her – she mused on Lord Derby's warmness towards her which did seem apparent.

CHAPTER 15

The next day was Sunday and Nancy believed that she should have Sunday afternoon free. However, she knew now about the picnic and felt that she should accompany the children if they were to attend.

However, as she awoke and dressed, Mrs Chapman entered without knocking.

"Breakfast is as usual in the nursery," she volunteered. "Many guests wish to attend Chapel which is adjoined to the main house. A curate takes the service when required. Lord Derby wishes the girls to attend and specifically asked that you be with them. The service will commence at ten o'clock."

Nancy hastened to the nursery where the girls were still eating breakfast. Mrs Compton had obviously dressed them. Nancy joined in and as she did so, Lord Derby appeared at the door.

"Has Mrs Chapman given you the message?"

"Yes, my Lord, we are to attend service in the chapel."

"Please be ready by nine-thirty. I will fetch you myself."

After breakfast and chatting to the girls, Nancy returned to her room for the bonnet. As she returned to the nursery, Lord Derby was waiting.

"It is nine-thirty. Come, let us be on our way."

Nancy and the girls followed Lord Derby from the main building to the chapel at the far end. Many guests were mingling about outside, the ladies no doubt to show off their bonnets and gowns.

Lord Derby greeted them and then ushered the girls and Nancy inside.

"We have our own private pew," he offered, and led them to a heavily carved oak pew near to the pulpit.

The other guests attending entered. Nancy heard one voice say, "Look at that," and guessed that it was Mrs Burstow indignant that she, Nancy, was in a private pew.

The service proceeded and the sermon was about forgiveness, using the parable of the Prodigal Son as an example.

At the end of the service, Nancy had no idea who was playing the organ, which was harmonious.

Nancy was greeted by the curate, who welcomed her. He addressed Lord Derby and the girls and then continued to speak to some of the guests.

Many guests of course acknowledged Lord Derby and some of the ladies when they were well away from chapel, gathered round and praised the children's gowns. No one spoke to Nancy and it was as if she did not exist.

Mrs Burstow came bustling up with Isobelle in tow.

"My Lord, do you not think my daughter's bonnet remarkable? I had it especially bespoke for the occasion."

"Your daughter does look charming," Lord Derby replied, "but I must get myself back to the main house. I am sure that you have been informed that Sunday lunch will today be at one o'clock, so please avail yourself of a walk in the grounds, or maybe a short rest in your rooms before lunch."

Mrs Burstow obviously felt rather snubbed but persisted. "My daughter could take your girls for a SAFE walk," she emphasised.

"How kind, but I am taking the girls back myself. Do feel free to enjoy yourself."

Lord Derby turned towards the main house, and Nancy and the girls followed.

"I wish you all to join in with the picnic this afternoon, that of course includes you, Nancy."

"Oh it will be such fun," exclaimed Emily. "We haven't been on a picnic for ages."

"We will be leaving at three o'clock," Lord Derby stated. "I suggest the girls wear something less formal. Mrs Compton will see to that."

Anna muttered, "I don't like Mrs Compton," but this was whispered.

Once back in the house, Nancy amused the children until their lunch at twelve as usual. After this was cleared away, Mrs Compton took the children away to change and Nancy returned to her room. She decided to put on her grey gown, as she was unsure where they would be seated at the picnic.

Nancy could see footmen and servants carrying tables, rugs and baskets, followed by the guests who were all laughing and chattering.

Again, Lord Derby was outside her door when she prepared to fetch the children, and indicated that they all follow him.

It was a short walk to the edge of the woods and already the rugs were down, the tables laid and there was food aplenty.

The servants served the guests and attended to their needs. Nancy and the children were also seated.

"I don't know why you are here," Mrs Burstow uttered. "Surely it should be Mrs Compton, the children's nurse, who should be with them."

Lord Derby heard the remark. "Madam, I have just hired a governess. The children need more than a nurse now."

One lady tutted. "Well, Lord Derby, maybe you will soon take a wife."

Mrs Burstow rallied on this. "Of course he will and then have children of his own. The girls could go to a convent school as the new Lady Derby would have her own family to consider."

Anna spoke up: "Uncle, I don't want to go away to a convent school. I want to stay here with you." She began to cry.

"So you shall, Anna, so you shall. Fear not, I love you both dearly."

Nancy put her arm around Anna as everyone was partaking of the food.

Then Mrs Burstow pulled Isobelle to her feet. "Lord Derby, I am sure that Isobelle would like to walk to the edge of the woods with you. Can you oblige?"

Lord Derby had little choice but to take Isobelle by the arm and they walked off.

Anna had stopped crying, but Nancy could see that both girls were not happy.

"I think I shall take the girls back to the house," she announced to no one in particular.

Mrs Burstow just sniffed and no one appeared to be at all interested in their movements.

Nancy indicated to the children that they should leave and they moved away. Suddenly Lord Derby turned and saw them. Leaving Isobelle, he hurried over.

"Why are you leaving so suddenly?" he asked. "There are some excellent sweetmeats and puddings to be eaten."

Emily spoke: "Uncle, the ladies are nasty and Anna has cried as you know. We want to go back."

Lord Derby could not respond to this. He just nodded and continued with his walk with Isobelle. He soon got tired of her monosyllabic replies to his conversation and returned her to her mother.

He joined up with his old friends Lord Horton and Lord Clements, whose ladies were still partaking of the picnic food.

"You seem down, old fellow," commented Lord Horton.

"This whole weekend has been a disaster," retorted Lord Derby. "One thing after another. I did not realise that people could be so spiteful. The Burstow woman is trying her best to foist her daughter onto me, but lovely as she is, she is not for me. I shall be glad when the morning comes and they all leave."

"Does that include Lady Clements and my wife and myself?" queried his friend jovially.

"Of course not. The other women seem to have taken against Nancy my new governess and I cannot stand injustice."

"Your governess is a lovely looking girl," stated Lord Horton. "The women are just jealous and Lady Burstow fears that all her hopes may come to nought."

"Quite right on that," replied Lord Derby sharply. "Still, I must return to my guests."

So saying, he moved over to the group saying, "Please feel free to return to the house at your leisure. I have arranged a piano recital in the music room at five o'clock and the evening meal will be announced by the gong at the time of eighty-thirty. My footman and servants are here for you, but I must return to the house now to check that everything is as it should be."

Lord Derby turned and left.

CHAPTER 16

When Lord Derby returned to the house, he stopped on the way to talk to his steward Barstairs. "My previous governess wished part of her wages sent home, before she eloped with my footman. If Miss Farran wishes to send some money home, please make sure that Charles takes it each month to her address."

"Certainly, my Lord," agreed Barstairs.

Lord Derby entered the nursery where Nancy was still consoling his nieces.

"May I enquire if you wish any of your salary sent home?" he enquired.

"Indeed, I would like that," retorted Nancy. "Half of it each month if it pleases your Lordship."

"Charles will take it to your home," stated Lord Derby. "I will leave your remaining wages in an envelope on the hall table each month. No one will touch that."

Nancy felt grateful again for his consideration.

"I am sorry that my nieces and your good self were upset by my guests. I am going to put a little more money in the envelope as reparation. I must now join the guests who will be arriving back at the house. Enjoy the rest of your evening." He turned to his nieces. "Remember, Emily and

Anna, that I loved my brother dearly and I also love you dearly. Remember that." Lord Derby left the room.

The servants brought in some food and drink for the children and Nancy, but Mrs Compton made a great show of preparing the children for bed, so Nancy once again retreated to her room. She could hear the sound of music as well as singing and thought Lord Derby must have also employed the services of a solo soprano.

Suddenly, Nancy heard screaming and crying coming from the children's bedroom. She hastily got up and ran to their room. Mrs Compton was smacking Anna and she was crying. Emily was screaming, "She couldn't help it, she couldn't help it."

"Whatever is the matter?" asked Nancy angrily. "Stop hitting the child."

"She's done it before," Emily stated. "But we have said nothing."

"Surely you could have told your other governess?"

"She said it was nothing."

"It isn't nothing." Nancy turned to Mrs Compton. "What has Anna done to deserve such treatment?"

"I am getting old and tired I suppose," admitted Mrs Compton. "She has been sick over her best dress."

"The child couldn't help it. There was some unpleasantness at the picnic which probably upset her. Both of them actually."

Nancy fetched a damp cloth and wiped away the little mess there was.

"I suggest you go to bed, Mrs Compton. Even if you are tired you should not take it out on the children. Perhaps you should ask Lord Derby if you may retire. I am sure that he would give you a pension."

Nancy helped the sobbing child to the bed and gave both girls a cuddle.

Mrs Compton, now crying herself, left the room and Nancy sat on the bed with both girls in her arms.

Suddenly, again, Lord Derby appeared. "Mason informed me that there appeared to be a problem. But I see that the girls are happy here with you."

Nancy did not like to make trouble, but Anna spoke up.

"Mrs Compton hit me. She has been getting more cross lately."

Lord Derby was aghast. "Is this correct?" he said to Emily.

"Yes, Uncle, we didn't like to make trouble. She was fine when Mama and Papa were alive, but she always seems to be in a bad mood these days."

Nancy spoke up. "I think Mrs Compton is getting old. Anna was only slightly sick on her newest dress and it has sponged off."

Lord Derby looked thoughtful. "I don't think the girls need a nurse any longer. I will find a maid servant to help them dress and into bed. I will pension Mrs Compton off. I believe she has a sister to whom she could go."

He looked at Nancy. "You always seem to help at the right moment. I am deeply in your debt."

Anna spoke up: "I love Nancy."

Emily added, "We both do. We are so pleased that she is here."

Lord Derby smiled. "As I am," he retorted, "as I am."

"I will leave you girls together." Although it was a single bed, the children stayed cuddled up to Nancy.

"May we come to your big bed?" asked Anna.

Nancy smiled. "You may," she said. All three went to Nancy's room, snuggled up and fell asleep.

Later Lord Derby, noticing the children were not in their room, gently opened Nancy's door. His heart felt like bursting when he saw all three asleep.

CHAPTER 17

Lord Derby was pensive when he left Nancy's room with the girls either side of her. He realised that he was thinking about her more than perhaps he should. Who was she really? She spoke well and had excellent deportment. For a fleeting moment he wondered if she could fill the role of Lady Derby, but he realised that he really knew little about the real Nancy. Yes, she was learned and educated, but who was she really?

On impulse he sent a message to Charles to be ready with the carriage the next morning. He knew that the girls would be well looked after and asked Mrs Chapman to allocate Gladys to be Nancy's maid servant. This caused a few eyebrows to be raised, but Lord Derby's word was law. Mrs Compton would soon be with her sister and the steward, Barstairs, had made all the financial arrangements.

The next morning Lord Derby asked Charles to take him to Nancy's cottage. Of course Charles now knew the way. He also took Mason with him.

When they reached the cottage, Lord Derby asked Mason to knock at the door. He had already guessed that it would be a small place after Nancy, like the governess before her, had asked the steward to send part of her wages and Charles had been designated to do so.

Mason returned stating that there was no reply. Lord Derby guessed that Nancy's brothers would be at the village school, but where was Mrs Ferran? He told Charles to take the carriage to the nearest shop. He knew that gossip spread like wildfire in these parts. True to form, the shopkeeper stated that Mary was working in the laundry at a nearby large house. The shopkeeper gave directions.

Once again, Charles took the carriage to the address and directed Mason to ask the owner if Mrs Ferran could step out.

As the carriage with Lord Derby's crest could clearly be seen, Mary was allowed to step outside.

Lord Derby invited her into the carriage, but she was bemused, wearing her working clothes and a large white apron.

"What do you do here, my dear?" he enquired.

"I am now a full-time laundress here. Luckily I have nearly finished the ironing of yesterday's washing. Is there any trouble with Nancy?"

"No, my dear. How much do they pay you?"

"Why, six shillings a week, my Lord."

"Mason," said Lord Derby, "go inside and state that Mrs Ferran cannot return."

Mary gasped. "I need the money, my Lord. I have two boys to support."

Lord Derby smiled. "My steward will send the equivalent money with Charles. You do not need to work now. I hold Nancy, your daughter, in the highest regard already. I feel there is more to this history than I know. Now tell me how all this has come about. You too speak well, as does Nancy. There is a mystery here, I can feel it."

Mary blushed. "My parents are Mr and Mrs Wakefield. They live at Thornton in Coventry. I have a brother, Bertram."

Lord Derby frowned. "I have heard of Bertram Wakefield. He is a known gambler."

"I fell in love with Antonio Ferran, my father's valet, and fell pregnant with Nancy. My father sent us away to the cottage. Unfortunately, my husband died and we had difficulty in surviving. Even the farmer for whom he worked became feeble. Nancy was and is clever and did well in the village school where she eventually taught. I also have twins aged nearly nine now."

"I think I know the large house Thornton. How could your parents treat you so. Your father was always a rich merchant?"

"I grew up in a lovely house," said Mary. "I had a governess and all that I could wish for. But my father was obstinate and even my mother Georgina could not change him."

"This is ridiculous," scoffed Lord Derby. "Most unjust. Now let me return you home and you certainly do not need to do laundry for others again."

Lord Derby told Charles to take them back to the cottage. He did not enter but he could see that there was a herb garden and the windows gleamed. It was indeed a pretty cottage, but still needed maintenance.

Lord Derby said that his steward would be in touch via Charles and turned to leave.

"Give Nancy my love," called Mary.

"Indeed I will," replied Lord Derby.

Lord Derby waved goodbye and instructed Charles to take them to Thornton in Coventry.

When the carriage arrived, Mr Wakefield was about to enter the house himself.

Mason was sent to enquire if Lord Derby could visit. Mr Wakefield was overwhelmed and a parlour maid came out immediately to usher Lord Derby inside. Mr Wakefield appeared to have no butler, but the house was indeed impressive as were the grounds.

Lord Derby was shown into the library and drinks were poured.

"To what do I owe the pleasure of your company?" Mr Wakefield asked.

"Well, it is about your family," answered Lord Derby.

As he spoke the library door opened and Georgina was about to enter, full of excitement at their esteemed visitor. But on hearing Lord Derby's remark, she hastily withdrew.

"W... Well, my Lord," Mr Wakefield almost stuttered. "May I enquire why my family is any concern of yours?"

Lord Derby smiled wryly. "Your granddaughter, Nancy, is governess to my nieces. I wished to know a little of her background. I discovered your daughter Mary, working as a laundress, an occupation I would have thought hardly suitable for a child of yours. Also, I am afraid to say, I have now realised that a perpetual gambler, Bertram Wakefield, is your son. It is alleged that he is deeply in debt."

Mr Wakefield's face paled; he mentioned Bertram first. "You are correct about my son, he has been asking for more money from myself and it is now a great concern. My daughter, Mary, however, disgraced herself and has had to live with the consequences. Why isn't her ne'er do well of a husband (I presumed they married at least) helping her?"

"I am afraid he died," Lord Derby answered. "I have spoken to your daughter and briefly heard the sorry tale. Your granddaughter Nancy is a bright and clever young lady. You also have twin grandsons aged nearly nine. You have not only cast away your daughter, but also the chance of being with three lovely grandchildren."

Mr Wakefield was silent. "Where is Mary working as a laundress?" he asked.

"I value Nancy highly and could not see her mother working thus. She is now permanently back at the cottage, but she should be here with you."

Mr Wakefield staggered a little. He poured himself another drink as Lord Derby's glass was still nearly full.

"Perhaps I have been foolish," confessed Mr Wakefield. "I will send for Mary and my grandsons. My wife Georgina will, I know, be delighted. I can do nothing about Bertram. I am afraid that we have over-indulged him. If I cut off his allowances, he will only get further into debt. But what about Nancy?"

Suddenly, Mr Wakefield's face had a knowing look. "You seem overly interested in the girl."

"She is doing a wonderful job with my nieces, who are my late brother's children. I am deeply grateful to her. I confess I have developed a very high regard for her, but that is all at the present time."

Mr Wakefield decided to let the matter drop.

Lord Derby continued, "I offered to re-imburse Mary's wages as a laundress, but if she is returning to your care, then I leave everything in your hands. She is your daughter and should not be in need."

"You may be right, my Lord," Mr Wakefield said humbly. "Thank you for all your concern, I will act immediately, but does Nancy not wish also to return here?"

"I know not," replied Lord Derby. "I will give her all of the facts and it is for her to make the decision. Now I must be on my way." Lord Derby left by the door which was opened by the parlour maid.

He just indicated to Charles and Mason that they were to return home.

CHAPTER 18

Nancy had heard that Lord Derby had left the house, and continued the day as usual with the children. She was amazed that she now had Gladys as a personal maid, as she was so used to fending not only for herself, but for others.

The day progressed and she had heard that Lord Derby was back in residence. The children were in bed when Mason scratched at her door. When Nancy opened the door he apologised for the intrusion but said that Lord Derby wished to see her in the library at her convenience.

Nancy did not hesitate. She smoothed her hair and without calling for Gladys went immediately to the library. She was concerned because Lord Derby looked serious.

"Please sit down, Nancy," he said. "And let me pour you a glass of cordial."

Nancy obeyed and took the glass with some trepidation.

"This has been a strange day," Lord Derby commented. "I may have been presumptuous, but I wished to know more of your family. You are so well spoken that I felt there was more to your background and maybe I should know of this."

Nancy gasped. Lord Derby continued. "I asked Charles to take me to your home. I eventually found your mother laundering. I realised that this work was not suitable as from her demeanour, she appeared a lady of quality. To cut a long story short, I encouraged her to close such work and offered to reimburse her wages. It was probably all on impulse, but she seemed so out of place laundering for another. Your mother told me some of her story and of her background. I found Mr Wakefield and I believe he sincerely regrets his previous actions. Not only had he lost a daughter, but three grandchildren. He has offered for you all to live at Thornton."

"But there is Bertram upon whom he dotes," interjected Nancy.

"Sadly, Bertram is in serious trouble with gambling and in dark territory. I fear that your grandfather may have to pay out a great deal of money to save him from the debtor's prison."

Nancy felt faint. Lord Derby continued. "You now may return to Thornton to be with your mother and brothers who will, I hope, now, lead the life into which your mother was born."

Nancy was silent for a moment then spoke. "I love it here, Lord Derby. I love the girls so much already. May I not stay?"

Lord Derby heaved a sigh of relief. "I so hoped to hear you say that. I can see that my nieces would be most disturbed if you left. Now that we no longer need to send half of your wages to your mother, it will be left each month directly, beside your bed on the bed table. Money, however, cannot recompense the love that you are giving to my nieces."

Nancy smiled at this. "We are happy," she said. "I wish to stay. My grandfather treated my mother abominably, but if returning to her old home makes her happy then so be it. Anyway, I must return to my room." Nancy smiled and left.

As she went to ascend the stairs, suddenly her foot caught in the hem of her dress. She felt herself falling, but she was quickly caught by Lord Derby who appeared to have followed her out of the library. As he caught her, Lord Derby could not restrain himself. He kissed her gently on the cheek and caressed it as he did so. Nancy did not pull away and within minutes they were in a close cuddle and Lord Derby was squeezing her tightly.

"I am afraid that I am falling in love with you," he said.

"You cannot be in love with a governess," answered Nancy sadly.

"Your grandparents are Mr and Mrs Wakefield," replied Lord Derby. "They own Thornton, a very splendid residence. In fact, you could be there now."

Nancy stepped away from Lord Derby's embrace.

"Apparently so, but I prefer to be with Emily and Anna."

At that moment there was a commotion at the front of the house and voices were raised.

"What on earth," gasped Lord Derby, but as he spoke, Harrison the butler was being pushed along by Mr Burstow. Mr Burstow stopped and said curtly to Lord Derby, "Take me into your library." Puzzled, Lord Derby gave Nancy an appealing look and turned towards the library. Nancy continued up the stairs towards her room, her head full of unanswered questions.

Did Lord Derby hope by his actions to persuade her to stay and look after his nieces? Did he wish to make her his mistress? Was it just an unexplained impulse? Could he, would he, ever consider marriage? If he did so, would it affect his own position in society?

Musing this, Nancy did not ring for Gladys or any maid, but undressed herself and went into the lovely fluffy bed.

Meanwhile, Lord Derby and Mr Burstow were now in the library.

"To what reason do you have to force yourself into my home?" enquired Lord Derby.

"My wife has sent me," muttered Mr Burstow. "To ask what are your intentions towards my daughter, Isobelle?"

"Surely if I had intentions," interrupted Lord Derby, "I would be visiting you.

"Well you walked alone with my daughter at the picnic," insisted Mr Burstow.

"Yes, at the suggestion of your wife. And as a gentleman I could hardly refuse. We were also always in full sight of those at the picnic. As it was, the walk was very short."

"Well, my wife considers that Isobelle has been compromised and that an offer of marriage should be forthcoming."

"Absolute rubbish," expostulated Lord Derby. "A very short walk in the full view of many is hardly a compromise. I am very sorry, Mr Burstow, but I have no intention of making an offer of marriage to your daughter. She is very beautiful, and I am sure will receive many suitable marriage offers. I have no notion of marriage at this moment. My duty is to my late brother, and to ensure that my nieces Emily and Anna are well cared for."

Mr Burstow would not be silenced. "My daughter Isobelle would make an excellent wife for you and could care for the children. Better, I am sure, than that governess you employ."

"Your daughter should have her chance of balls and social events," Lord Derby insisted. "My present governess is well qualified to educate the children in a manner that satisfies me. Now, Mr Burstow, please return to your carriage which I am sure is outside. Harrison will see you out."

Harrison and Mason magically appeared either side of the library door.

Mr Burstow had no choice but to turn and leave. He did so with no farewell, and exited with an angry face.

Lord Derby was left thinking. Could he marry Nancy? He had met her mother and her grandparents, and they certainly had a grand residence, but they had an addicted gambler for a son. Perhaps he could ruin them. Although he had regretted his interaction with the local gentry, he wondered if it was indeed time that he took a wife. Perhaps he should go about this thought in a different way. Perhaps he should give a ball and send invitations to all local gentry with eligible daughters, but definitely not Isobelle Burstow. Pondering on this thought, he sent for his valet and retired for the night.

CHAPTER 19

Almost immediately, the next day in fact, Lord Derby
instructed his steward, Barstairs, to have invitations
printed to all the local gentry within a radius of ten miles.
He knew that Barstairs could research this. Fairstow
had a large ballroom which had fallen into neglect. He
instructed Barstairs to organise workmen to refurbish this
and to organise musicians for a ball in four weeks from the
previous Saturday. He told Mrs Chapman to again have
rooms prepared for guests.

Nancy heard of all this activity, apart from instructing
workmen coming and going, in the house from Gladys who
was now definitely her personal maid.

Nancy was rather bewildered because she had
understood that Lord Derby had regretted his weekend
with neighbours. She had not, however, heard of Mr
Burstow's visit. Lord Derby was warm and courteous to
her, visiting the school room on various occasions, but
there were no more invitations to tete-a-tete meetings and
certainly no more cuddles. Meals were as usual in the
nursery/school room, but Nancy, Emily and Anna were
happy. The children could now write in cursive writing
and their reading was excellent. There was an abundance

of children's books and full advantage was taken of these.

The children had a private dressmaker who visited regularly and either let down hems, or made new gowns for them. Nancy now had the full use of all her salary and occasionally, with Lord Derby's permission, would be taken to the village dressmaker, who made Nancy a couple of simple but slightly more elaborate gowns. She also had slippers made by the local cobblers.

The time came for the Friday before the ball. The house was decorated with greenery and flowers and when Nancy peeped in, the ballroom looked magnificent. Murals on the ceiling had been repainted, statues regilded, and settees and sofas refurbished in gold and velvet. The floor shone and the candelabra were gleaming.

The guests were due to arrive on the Saturday evening for the ball at eight o'clock. The children were to be in bed. Lord Derby, however, suddenly appeared at the school room door at their teatime.

"I hope you will be attending the ball, Nancy," he declared.

Nancy blushed. "I hardly think it is in keeping, my Lord. I do have new gowns now, but nothing suitable for a ball of this magnitude."

Lord Derby did not offer help in this instance but said, "I am sure that one of your gowns would suffice. I would like you to attend." He turned and left.

Nancy was nonplussed. She did have another pale blue gown, that perhaps could be decorated.

Gladys, when told, was willing to help. She went into the village and purchased some blue satin ribbons and rosettes on the Saturday morning and industriously stitched and sewed during the afternoon.

Nancy attended to the children and explained that she was to attend the ball. The children were excited for her and she promised to recount all the next day.

Gladys helped her into the newly decorated gown and wove flowers into her loosened hair. Nancy looked lovely. Gladys had purchased long gloves for her on her behalf and she already had slippers.

There was much noise from the carriages and horses and most guests were to return home after the event. However, as stated, a few rooms were readied for guests unable or unwilling to make the journey home.

Nancy decided to enter the ballroom at nine o'clock. The Master of Ceremonies announced all the guests, but Nancy just slipped in and sat down.

The musicians were playing for a cotillion and Nancy watched, fascinated.

She expected to be a wallflower all evening, but suddenly Lord Derby appeared and smilingly asked her for the next dance, a quadrille. Nancy blushingly accepted.

As the cotillion ended, Lord Derby escorted Nancy onto the floor. Nancy could hear whispers and then – oh not again. Mrs Burstow (who appeared to have invited herself and her daughter) could be heard saying, "What a dreadful dress that girl is wearing." Nancy and Lord Derby danced and ignored this loud remark.

Suddenly, Mason appeared at Lord Derby's side. "My Lord, Mr Burstow is unwell and in the library. He has asked for help."

Lord Derby and Nancy completed the dance and Lord Derby escorted Nancy back to her seat. He hastened to the library. Inside was not Mr Burstow, but Isobelle, fanning herself on the velvet couch. The door slammed.

Nancy had heard Mason's cri de coeur and decided to help. The library door was closed but she opened it.

Inside was Lord Derby looking rather frantic with Isobelle Burstow smiling. Nancy entered, the door behind was thrown back and Mrs Burstow and a companion entered.

"You have compromised my daughter. You must offer marriage," she shrieked.

"I am here," Nancy intermitted.

Mrs Burstow had failed to notice this.

Nancy continued, "I am sure your daughter wished to view the library and maybe borrow a book to take home. However, I feel that she is missing the ball and would prefer to return to the ballroom."

Mrs Burstow realised that her cunning plan had failed.

"Come, daughter," she said, "let us partake of some refreshments." They left.

Lord Derby looked at Nancy. "How can I thank you? You have saved me from ignominy or total catastrophe. You are always there when I need you."

He put his hands onto her shoulders, "I cannot help it. I love you. I called this ball to find a wife, but again I know in my heart it is a waste of time. Nancy, it is you that I love. Nancy, it is you that I want as my wife. We will return to the ball and I will act as a host should, but I know that none of the young girls here will hold my heart. I will visit your grandfather tomorrow and ask his permission to wed you. I will then get a special licence and we can be married immediately by my chaplain in the manorial chapel."

Nancy was overwhelmed. Yes, she had certainly developed strong feelings for Lord Derby.

"Yes, I will marry you because I sense in you a great kindness, particularly to your nieces whom I have come to love. But it is ridiculous in that I do not even know your first name."

"Maximilian," replied Lord Derby, smiling happily at her agreement.

The ball progressed with Mr Burstow and his family leaving. They had not been invited, but when they heard of others who had, decided that it must be an oversight. Perhaps they were so full of their own importance, rules ceased to exist.

Most guests departed that night with many disappointed Mamas taking their offspring with them. The remaining few left the next morning, as did Lord Derby to Thornton House.

Mr Wakefield received him with trepidation, but was amazed at the reason for his visit. He readily agreed to the marriage of course as it would send his credibility in society rocketing, and may even help his son Bertram.

Lord Derby asked to speak to Mary, which was of course permitted, and Lord Derby confessed the reason for the visit.

Mary was happily settled into Thornton House as were the two boys. Mr Wakefield had obviously tried to make amends for his harsh and previously cruel behaviour. Lord Derby assured her that she and the boys would always be welcome at Fairstow Manor.

CHAPTER 20

True to his word, Lord Derby rapidly obtained the special licence and he and Nancy were married within days. Only Lord Derby's best friends, Lord and Lady Horton and Lord and Lady Clements, were present as witnesses. Lord Derby's sister was once again away on a tour of Europe.

Nancy had no time to prepare a wedding dress, but wore the dress that Gladys had so diligently worked on for the ball, even though it had been sneered at by the ever spiteful Mrs Burstow. The gardener had given her a lovely posy of fresh flowers to hold as she walked down the aisle alone.

Mr and Mrs Wakefield were notified but Lord Derby found it hard to forgive their previous treatment of Nancy's mother. They were informed that the marriage was taking place, but no invitation was issued. Mr Wakefield realised why. Mary had received an invitation, but she too felt that perhaps she was in some way to blame for Nancy's hard life and felt that she was not quite mentally adjusted to all that was happening. Via a messenger she did send her daughter all good wishes and love for her future happiness.

Because of the children, Nancy declined a honeymoon, but was naturally moved into the large bedroom next to

Lord Derby, which had a connecting door.

Nancy was quite innocent in the matter of consummation of the marriage, but she had always felt a magnetic attachment to Lord Derby, who was indeed a handsome man. He had had mistresses since his twenties and was now thirty-two years of age. None of his former loves had caught his attention permanently and had only been very brief affairs. He realised that Nancy would be a virgin, but on their wedding night he skilfully introduced her to the art of love and Nancy was thrilled with the lovemaking, after only a brief moment of discomfort.

Waking on the morning after their wedding, she smiled at Lord Derby.

"I am the happiest man in the world," he said.

"I too am happy," replied Nancy. "I must go to the children."

It had been thought that as there was so little time for preparation that the children would not attend.

They had, however, been invited to the wonderful spread that Mrs Chapman and the staff had put out on the dining table. They had been looked after by the faithful Gladys. They had been so happy that their governess whom they loved, was now their aunt and in reality a surrogate mother. Nancy did not wish for another governess to take her place, but as all household duties were well undertaken by the staff, only had to give approval to menus and such.

All the family now ate at the regular times in the dining room and menus were adapted for the children.

Mary was eventually encouraged to visit with the boys, conveyed by Charles in the carriage that initially took Nancy to her present home.

Mary stayed for four weeks and the chaplain, when introduced to her, was obviously very enamoured. The chaplain did have his own large inherited house and the romance appeared to be progressing well. Nancy felt sure that in time she and the family may be attending a wedding.

Mr and Mrs Wakefield did attend some evening suppers, but Mr Wakefield's health was deteriorating. Noticing this, the renegade son Bertram ceased his prodigious gambling and amazingly settled into assisting in the running of Thornton. Much of the original business in trade, silks and spices had gradually died away, but Mr Wakefield was still a very wealthy man. Bertram had been spoiled yet again by his father paying off his creditors, but was now repaying such largesse by taking onto his shoulders the responsibility of Thornton.

Nancy continued with the girls' education and even after giving birth to a baby boy, named Edmund, still found time for the girls, but employed a nurse for the baby.

Nancy did not entertain a great deal because her life was devoted to the children she called daughters, and of course Edmund.

The household ran smoothly but Nancy never forgot the hardship her mother and brothers, plus herself, had endured after the death of Antonio. She always helped anyone with hardship in the village.

CHAPTER 21

Nancy was very happy indeed and everyone was most respectful to the new Lady Derby. Maximillian was overjoyed with his baby son and everything was going very smoothly until one day Nancy noticed that when Charles dropped her off in the village to enable her to purchase some new ribbons for a gown, two ladies refused to look at her or speak as she passed.

She noticed that the drapery shop was full of women, but when she smiled brightly and said, "Good Morning," there was a stony silence. Even the proprietress seemed strangely unhelpful. Nancy purchased some gold and blue ribbon and returned to the carriage.

She decided to speak to Charles.

"The villagers do not appear friendly today," she commented.

Charles hesitated before moving the horses.

"There have been some ugly rumours, madam," he at last said reluctantly.

"Rumours. About what?" enquired Nancy.

"I cannot say, madam," replied Charles, and the carriage moved forward to return home to Fairstow Manor.

Nancy sat within the carriage puzzled.

"What on earth could cause ugly rumours," she pondered. She was legally wed. She had done nothing wrong. Even the incident with Thomas Burstow had been cleared up. She had had no problems with the staff. She was totally bewildered.

"Could Lord Derby have had a vindictive mistress," she mused, but there had been no evidence of any such occurrence. Lord Derby had always seemed too busy with the manor and his nieces. She knew that in this part of the country, people had very high standards, particularly manifested between the rich and the poor. The resentment of the poorer classes could cause problems, but the ladies with whom she had come into contact were perfectly respectable matrons with their younger daughters.

When she alighted from the carriage she immediately went into the library to find Lord Derby.

He smiled at her happily. "Did you enjoy your shopping expedition?" he asked.

"Something strange happened today," stated Nancy. "The women appeared to shun me and even Charles admitted, albeit reluctantly, that there had been some ugly rumours."

"What nonsense is this?" exclaimed Lord Derby angrily. "How dare anyone show anything but the greatest respect to my wife. Go and prepare for lunch, my love. I will sort this stupidity out at once."

He kissed Nancy fondly on the cheek and as she exited the room, he asked Mason to send for Charles at once.

Charles soon arrived at the library, still in his coachman's gear.

"What is this about rumours?" asked Lord Derby in a sharp tone.

"I am sorry, my Lord, but I heard it from a stable lad."

"Heard what?" demanded Lord Derby, getting more annoyed.

"It is being put about, my Lord, that Lady Derby is illegitimate and therefore should have no credibility as a lady."

"Stuff and nonsense," scoffed Lord Derby. "Even if she was the lowest vagabond, as my wife she should command respect, but the accusation is entirely false. Who could have started such a fallacy?"

"I believe the perpetrator is Mrs Burstow my Lord. The story has come out that Mr Wakefield's daughter Mary, ran off with an Italian valet, Antonio, and that Lady Derby is the result of such a union."

"I know all the history of my wife's childhood," snorted Lord Derby. "In fact, Lady Derby's mother is now back at Thornton House with her father and mother."

"That is known, my Lord," retorted Charles, "but Mrs Burstow is stating that they lived like paupers in a cottage, and that Lady Derby's mother and father were unwed."

"I can find the priest that married them," spat Lord Derby, "and will have the chaplain confirm it in church if it is the last thing that I do. It is a disgrace, and unworthy of Mrs Burstow. She is just bitter because she wanted me to marry her own daughter Isobelle."

"My Lord, would it not be better to let the matter rest. It is probably only a storm in a teacup," ventured Charles.

"It is no storm in a teacup if insult is offered to my wife," retorted Lord Derby. "Maybe asking the chaplain to clear up the matter in church is a bridge too far, but I will go to the parish priest who married them myself and ask to borrow the register."

Still fuming, Lord Derby dismissed Charles and then prepared himself for lunch. Lady Derby had been to see that all was well with baby Edmund, and Emily and Anna were ready for lunch.

During the meal Lord Derby made no mention of the incident, neither did Nancy.

The girls felt the strangeness in the atmosphere and as they now considered Nancy their mother, Emily ventured to ask, "Is all well, Mama?"

"Fine, my dear," responded Nancy. "Nothing for you two girls to bother your heads about."

CHAPTER 22

After the meal, Lord Derby went to the stables and chose the horse Persephone to ride. Persephone was an Arab Stallion and very fleet of foot. He rode hastily to Merridon and soon found the priest. He explained the situation and the priest soon found the register which incorporated the words of the marriage between Mary and Antonio. The priest was reluctant to part with such a valuable document but after Lord Derby promised him much recompense, he capitulated, stating that it could be loaned for a day, as further weddings in that neighbourhood were due.

Lord Derby thanked him profusely and planned that his coachman, Charles, would return it within hours.

Lord Derby rode Persephone to Mr and Mrs Burstow's house. He did not knock at the door nor wait for any servant to open it. He burst into the hall and entered the drawing room. There were several guests present and Mr Burstow was leaning against the fireplace nonchalantly. He of course recognised Lord Derby, and standing upright enquired brusquely the meaning of such a hasty intrusion.

"Your wife," snarled Lord Derby, "has been spreading rumours that my wife is illegitimate. That her mother and father were unmarried. If she had been illegitimate, it would have bothered me not. She was wonderful to my two nieces before we wed, and I fell in love with her. She means everything in the world to me and always will do. However, here is the parish register which proves that her parents were indeed married." He thrust the register at Mr Burstow.

Mrs Burstow was reclining on a settee. Lord Derby waited for Mr Burstow to see the register and then thrust it in front of Mrs Burstow.

"Here is indisputable evidence (although it would matter to me not), that my wife's mother and father were married. What malice has caused you to spread such a malicious and untrue rumour and how shallow are your compatriots to give credence to such rubbish."

"How dare you speak so to my wife," Mr Burstow complained.

"How dare your wife spread such malice," retorted Lord Derby. "Whatever background my wife had is of no significance because she is Lady Derby. But the lies have spread and festered in the village like a plague, even my stable lads had apparently heard it. It is slander and I could bring you, Mrs Burstow, before a magistrate for defamation of character that would make you the laughing stock of the village."

Mrs Burstow paled, and put her hand to her head.

"I am so sorry, I was mistaken."

"No. You were driven by sheer spite," uttered Lord Derby, "and I have no wish to ever see you or your family at Fairstow Manor. The problem is that now the rumour has spread, I am unsure how it can be corrected. My wife's mother has her marriage lines, but I would not demean her to ask her to produce them. This parish register has to be returned promptly as I have given my word it shall be so. The evil you have committed is beyond forgiveness."

Mrs Burstow said faintly, "I could tell my friends that I was mistaken."

"The rumour appears to be spread too far. I shall have to give a ball and make an announcement. I do not like large gatherings – the last at Fairstow was a disaster – but to do something I must. Madam, you are beneath contempt."

So saying, Lord Derby exited the house, slamming the door as he did so, again waiting for no help from the butler or footmen that were employed.

CHAPTER 23

As he rode Persephone home, Lord Derby pondered on the problem. If he gave a ball, in order to make a statement, he would have to have his steward send out invitations. What would happen if there were refusals?

He rode Persephone to the stables and asked Charles to immediately go to Merridon and return the register to the priest as promised.

He went into the library and considered the problem. He knew that village life engendered gossip, and bad news was almost relished to relieve the tedium of everyday life. He thought deeply and knew for certain that there would be refusals to a ball, even if Mrs Burstow made good her promise to correct the impression she had given to her friends and acquaintances that Lady Derby was illegitimate.

He thought yet again how small minded some people were, because for goodness' sake what did it matter. It is what a person is that should count, their own nature, their kindness or willingness to help others, their whole demeanour; but there it was. The damage had been done and as it concerned his wife, he had no doubt that it had spread like wildfire. Burning into people's brains and feeding on envy and jealousy.

He knew of only one way to solve this problem. He would call on the Bishop. He had known him for years as they had once been at a church school together, before Lord Derby went to Oxford.

The next day he checked with Charles that the register had been returned, and then asked him to take him to Bishop Angus's palace. Saying nothing beyond the banal to Nancy, and of course kissing her and the children, including baby Edmund, they set off. Maximillian had explained he would be away for a few days, visiting a friend, which was in essence true.

The Bishop's palace was in London and they made several stops along the way. Once there, Lord Derby explained to a servant that his need to see the Bishop was desperate. Immediately Bishop Angus offered him admittance and over a glass of sherry Lord Derby explained the problem.

Bishop Angus could see only one solution which he promised to try.

He explained that Queen Victoria was of course still grieving from Albert's death but could be sympathetic to the problem. She seldom went out, but just a brief appearance at the ball would ensure that all would attend. Queen Victoria was now fifty-seven, and had been a widow for almost twenty years, but Bishop Angus promised to do his best.

Lord Derby returned to Fairstow feeling at least there was some hope for a solution. He said nothing to Nancy but just waited for a messenger. He had told Bishop Angus that the ball would be two weeks on a Saturday.

Bishop Angus gained admission to the palace, where amazingly Queen Victoria was in residence, but of course dressed entirely in black. When Bishop Angus gained admittance to her presence, he explained the situation. Queen Victoria had of course been madly in love with Albert, and although grieving, a grief that never left her, was sympathetic to love.

She promised to appear briefly on the steps leading to the ballroom, but would then leave.

A messenger was sent to Lord Derby who immediately obtained the gilt-edged invitations for his steward, Barstairs, to address. Not of course to Mr and Mrs Burstow. It was mentioned on the invitation that Queen Victoria would appear as the trumpeters signalled the opening of the ball.

When Nancy was told, she was humbled by Lord Derby's efforts to put matters right. She had of course to now organise the ball and obtain the best musicians and decorate the ballroom in a manner fit for a Queen, although Queen Victoria would only be putting in a token appearance.

Barstairs mainly organised the majority of the preparations as did the housekeeper. Nancy approved the elaborate buffet of refreshments which included truffles, oysters, caviar, syllabubs and all delicacies.

CHAPTER 24

New gowns had to be hastily purchased by the ladies invited. The local dressmaker was overwhelmed with new orders, but Nancy had, by now, many lovely gowns sent for from London, given the right measurements, and had sent samples of fabrics and designs from which to choose. She decided on a silver and blue gown upon which she knew Lord Derby had complimented her. Invitations were sent to not only the local gentry, but to leading business personnel and manufacturers. Mr and Mrs Wakefield were invited as of course was Mary.

Lord Clements was now sadly a widower and Lord Derby decided to introduce him to Mary. Lord Clements had two boys of similar age to John and James, and Lord Derby thought Mary would make Lord Clements an ideal wife, and it would be good for her to leave the rather claustrophobic atmosphere of Thornton House. Mary had never really thought of the chaplain as the ideal husband.

Naturally, with the mention of Queen Victoria, all invitations were gladly accepted and gossip was rife. Why would Lord Derby organise a ball when his wife's name was tarnished, and why was Queen Victoria (known to now be a recluse), attending at all? The village and locals were all in a buzz of anticipation.

Emily and Anna had new gowns and they too were puzzled at the elaborate preparations for the ball. Baby Edmund had yet to be christened, but the ball could have nothing to do with such an event. Nancy continued to teach and guide them, but gave them no inclination of the gossip that had triggered such an event.

Lord Derby was overwhelmed at Queen Victoria's generosity of spirit to attend, even briefly, the ball he had caused to be organised. If anyone enquired why he was so doing it, was answered briefly in a few words, "For the love of my wife". No one could give any response to such a reply but take it as a tangible expression of the deep love he had for his wife.

However, Lord Derby was still unsure of how to undo the damage that had been done and how to quell the gossip. He was in a quandary. He could not embarrass his wife and her mother with any direct announcement. He decided that he would let Mrs Burstow's promise to refute the allegation to her friends and acquaintances stand, and that the mere presence of Queen Victoria at the ball should be sufficient to restore any smear on his wife's name. He was still inwardly furious that such nonsensical gossip had been accepted as fact and had obviously spread so rapidly. He knew that as a Lord he was held by some in awe, but had hoped that as a good landlord, and that his true kindness to his tenants would have upheld the good name not only of himself but of his wife. He mused ruefully that obviously some people would always hold some resentment of his wealth, title and status and this he should accept with good grace. It would not prevent him from being the fair and noble person he wished to be.

All of the invitations were accepted and Lord Derby ensured that Lord Clements was included. The next few days were full of activity, chandeliers cleaned, windows gleamed and floors polished. Lord Derby asked the housekeeper, Mrs Chapman, to employ more help to make the manor pristine.

CHAPTER 25

The day dawned. The musicians arrived early with their instruments and the tables at the end of the ballroom were already groaning with superb refreshments. Various drinks were of course available including ratafia (a liqueur flavoured with almonds or the kernels of peaches, apricots or cherries), wine and of course lemonade. At the time of eight o'clock carriages began to arrive and soon the ballroom was nearly full. The master of ceremonies announced the guests, who had to descend ten marble steps to the ballroom. Lord and Lady Derby stood beside the master of ceremonies. At exactly eight-thirty Queen Victoria arrived. She was heralded by six trumpeters. Everyone bowed or curtsied as she stood at the top of the steps, followed by her maids. After the fanfare there was total silence. Queen Victoria spoke briefly.

"I open this ball, to honour Lord and Lady Derby. I am sure that you will enjoy their hospitality. The ball is given as an homage to Lady Derby for her kindness to her husband's family and of course to the neighbourhood." She then turned and was escorted back to her carriage.

The visit, heralded much talk. It was a unique and unusual honour of the Queen to grace any event these days, let alone a ball given by a mere Lord and Lady. The musicians were excellent and the ball proceeded well. Lord Derby danced the first dance with Nancy and then left to introduce Mary to Lord Clements. Mary looked quite lovely. She had endured many stresses and strains and was approaching middle age now, but her gown of gold cloth and lace was spectacular, and her hair was burnished and shone. Lord Clements was himself nearing sixty, but he admired the grace and elegance of his newly introduced lady. He immediately offered to dance with her and Mary, being unknown, had several vacancies in her card. Lord Derby smiled secretly as it was apparent that his intuition had been correct and that they would form a friendship.

Nancy was delighted with the success of the ball, and of course was now surrounded by people willing to ingratiate themselves with someone who could persuade the Queen herself to open the ball. They did not know of course about the efforts of Bishop Angus, and the machinations that caused such a major event to occur.

Carriages took all guests back to their homes as Lord Derby was emphatic that no guest should stay the night at Fairstow Manor.

As the last guest departed there was a cry from the nursemaid. She came running down to Lady Derby. "Baby Edmund is hot and feverish," she gasped. "I think a doctor should be called."

Nancy and Maximillian immediately sent Mason for the doctor who amazingly was just getting into his carriage after the ball.

They rushed with the doctor to the nursery, where the nursemaid was wringing her hands and crying.

Doctor Fairfax, a new doctor in the village, looked at baby Edmund.

"Goodness!" he exclaimed. "The child only has some wind." He patted the child firmly on the back. Edmund gave a gulp and then a smile.

"Nothing to worry about," he ventured, before turning to the nursemaid. "I would have thought that you would have known, my dear," he said kindly. "But I suppose it is better to be safe than sorry."

The nursemaid flushed red. "I am sorry," she exclaimed. "I think all the excitement in the house about the ball got to my head. Of course I should have known how to deal with it."

"Never mind," said Lady Derby kindly. "All's well that ends well."

She turned to Doctor Fairfax. "I am so sorry that you have been troubled and that your coach had to wait."

"No problem, my lady," retorted Doctor Fairfax. "I am glad to have been of service, and may I add, the ball was wonderful. I am as yet unwed, and I had many dances with lovely ladies."

Lord Derby smiled. "Well I wish you well in that," he said. "May you find a wife with whom to be as happy as I."

With that the doctor left.

CHAPTER 26

he clearing up after the ball was soon completed on the Sunday by the extra hired helps. The ballroom was back to its pristine condition. The musicians had of course been paid by the steward and any remaining refreshments were taken down to the kitchen where they were received with relish.

When Nancy visited the village again to purchase some gloves that she had previously seen, normality had been restored and once again she was received with courtesy and respect.

On the way home, however, in the carriage being driven as usual by Charles, but with two grooms, plus the maids also in attendance, as she neared the manor she saw smoke rising in the distance.

Nancy leaned out of the window and pointed this out to Charles, who looked immediately concerned.

"Please drive faster," urged Nancy.

One of the maids began to shout, "It is near the house, my Lady."

Nancy did not reply, but as they neared the manor, they saw horses being led from the stables, and it was obvious that there was a serious fire.

"Stop the carriage," urged Nancy. "I must make sure my horse and Lord Derby's horse are safe. Get to the house immediately and inform Lord Derby."

Trees may have prevented the household from seeing the smoke, but as she spoke it obviously had been seen.

Lord Derby and all the male household were rushing to the stables. A line had been formed by the stable hands not leading out the horses, to pass buckets of water from the nearby stored pump.

Nancy could see that all the horses were being led out to a nearby field for safety and those involved in this were rushing back to help.

"Stay clear, my dear," called Lord Derby, when he saw Nancy. "The horses are safe. It looks as if one stable block is ruined but we are trying now to prevent further damage."

The burned stable block collapsed. Luckily there were no living quarters above this.

With speed and precision all the men passed the water quickly, saving the whole block from ruin.

As the last sparks died out, Lord Derby told the exhausted men to use a hydrant some distance away to clean up. If they were stable hands, the men from the house were to ask the female servants there to prepare hot water in order that they may be cleansed.

Lord Derby went over and thanked them all, presumably for their help, and said that any damaged clothing would be renewed at the earliest opportunity. He gave these instructions to his steward.

"I will bring in extra village help tomorrow to repair existing damage to the stables," he added. "And also obtain a builder to rebuild the burnt stable. We will leave the horses in the field today and see what can be salvaged for their return tomorrow. Please put extra hay and water in the field for them."

Before he left, however, he turned to his head stableman.

"How on earth did this catastrophe happen?" he enquired. "If it had been from one of the living quarters above the collapsed stable I could have guessed that could be the source, but there is no fire in that quarter."

"I am sorry to say, my Lord," replied the head man. "I saw Mr Burstow himself near the stable with a stable lad not known to myself. I thought he had come on an unusual visit and watched him, although he is a neighbour. The lad threw a torch into the stable which immediately ignited the hay and straw. I was about one hundred yards away and ran to the scene immediately. I recognised Mr Burstow from that distance as he always wears a deep red coat with many capes. It had ignited so quickly, my Lord, and my main concern was for the horses."

"Quite right," answered Lord Derby. "Do not fret. As I have said, it will all be put in order and restored. Fortunately, there is no loss of life or injury to the horses thanks to your fast response. Now I must be on my way. You will be recompensed for your prompt action."

"Thank you, my Lord. It is a pleasure to be in your service," answered the head man.

117

Lord Derby returned to the manor to check that all was well within. He mentioned to the housekeeper that due to the fire, and the inconvenience to the household, only a cold collation had to be spread in the dining room in buffet fashion. He knew that all kitchen staff and servants would be well looked after.

Nancy was with the girls and the nursemaid with Edmund. Lord Derby checked that all was well with them and reassured Nancy that all horses were well. There were dogs and cats in the stables, but they had made their own escape and would no doubt return.

Lord Derby had not changed his clothing, nor did he.

"I am going to the nearest magistrate," he informed Nancy.

Looking at his face, Nancy decided that it was best to say nothing.

Lord Derby stated, "I gather a cold collation is to be set up in the dining room for the rest of the day, so the girls and yourself may eat when you choose. I am unsure how long I shall be."

This was curtly spoken for Lord Derby, so all Nancy said was, "Take care, my love," and kissed him on the check.

Still in his begrimed clothing, Lord Derby strode to the field and took Persephone to the tack room which was fortunately unharmed. He saddled up himself and with no groom rode into Merridon.

He soon found the magistrate's office, and after being admitted, told of how Mr Burstow and a lad had been seen setting fire to his stables.

"This is very serious indeed," stated the magistrate. "I will send men at once to bring in Mr Burstow for questioning. We will hold him and the boy before passing him onto the High Supreme Court of Justice which was, as you know, created under the Jurisdiction Acts of 1873 and 1875. He will no doubt have the choice of a compensatory sentence or life imprisonment. The lad will no doubt get a birching, but leniency may be offered as he was under direct instructions apparently."

Lord Derby was satisfied with this and knew that since Sir Robert Peel (1788 – 1850) introduced 'Peelers' or 'Bobbies', some of these men performed extremely well. He returned home satisfied that he had done all that he could.

CHAPTER 27

The next day was busy, reorganising the building of the new stable, rehoming the horses in repaired stables, ordering new clothing for those concerned and generally keeping the situation calm.

The steward was a great help in this.

News filtered out that 'Peelers' or 'bobbies' newly formed had eventually taken Mr Burstow away to a cell before a court hearing, but the lad had been shown clemency.

When Nancy heard from her maid Gladys, all that had happened, she was frozen with shock. She then felt partly (albeit undeserved) sorry for Mrs Burstow but particularly for Isobelle. Whatever the court ruling on her father, it would do her prospects no favour in her pursuit of a husband.

There was too much work to be done, however, for her to muse too long on the matter.

What did delight her was that Lord Clements approached his friend Lord Derby stating that as a widower, he was very taken with Nancy's mother, and asked for his advice on the matter.

Lord Derby was happy to confirm that he had secretly hoped that this would occur and felt that Mary would be an ideal wife for his old friend. Lord Clements had a small but enchanting manor house and grounds two miles away, and was certainly financially comfortable from various inheritances.

Lord Derby told Nancy of the visit and she too was delighted for her mother. She enquired anxiously about the boys but was told that Lord Clements had two sons himself and would be happy to have an extended family.

Nancy did wonder how Mr and Mrs Wakefield would react to this turn of events.

In fact, when Lord Clements sent a card indicating a call, they were very delighted.

"We are being accepted completely into society," stated Mr Wakefield.

"Well, we really could not have been left out from the ball, but that was a single event. We must not build our hopes too high. We are fortunate that Mary has forgiven us for your harsh treatment, and I do so love her sons."

"Lord Clements is coming," commented Mr Wakefield, not wishing to be reminded of his previous dreadful behaviour. "We have risen in society, Nancy our granddaughter is married to a Lord and that sets us above others."

I do not wish to be set above," stated Georgina. "I just wish harmony to reign. You were wrong, husband, to send Mary and Antonio away all those years ago. It was not my wish. You turned your back on your own daughter."

"My God!" exclaimed Mr Wakefield. "She was pregnant. What was I to do?"

"Help them marry immediately. Antonio was a clever man, he could have had a position on your farm. There is and still is an empty dower house in these grounds. They could have lived there or even here."

"You dare to speak to me thus!" exclaimed Mr Wakefield.

"It should have been said many years before. I had to beg you to show any clemency."

Mr Wakefield's face went purple, but he knew that Georgina spoke only the truth.

Mr Wakefield had given permission of course for Lord Clements to call and received him comfortably in the library. He was happily thinking this was just a social visit, but was amazed when Lord Clements told him the true reason for his visit.

"I am enamoured with your daughter Mary," he stated. "I am sadly a widower and have two sons. I am financially solvent and have a small manor house called Thropston, which would be the better for a wife."

"You wish to offer for Mary," ejaculated Mr Wakefield. "Do you know of her past history?"

"Gossip spreads, and Lord Derby told me in confidence. Mr Wakefield, we will draw a blanket over your part in all the events. Now is now. Mary is a gentle soul, and I would be honoured if she would consent to be my wife."

Mr Wakefield spluttered and nearly choked but could only say to his servant, "Send for Mary!"

Mary soon entered and Mr Wakefield told her of Lord Clements' proposal.

Mary smiled. "It is only a brief acquaintance, at the ball and I must confess, Lord Clement has taken me from the village in his carriage. Such lightning things do happen and we seem most comfortable with each other. I will say yes."

Lord Clements laughed, and from his waistcoat pocket produced a large ruby and diamond ring which, grasping Mary's hand, he slid onto her ring finger.

Mary gasped at the beauty of the ring.

"Thank you for the honour, my Lord," she said.

"William," added Lord Clements smiling.

"William," also smiled Mary. "But we must have a slightly longer engagement so that we really do know and understand each other. Certainly, six months."

"I quite understand," said Lord Clements. "I shall call as often as possible and will of course show you your future home, Thropston. I will now take my leave."

Bowing to Mary and Mr Wakefield, he was escorted by a servant to the door.

Mr Wakefield was dumbfounded. He sent for a servant to fetch Georgina, leaving Mary to seat herself down on a chair looking with awe and wonder at the beautiful ring on her finger.

When Georgina heard the news, she cried tears of joy. "All has come right," she laughed. "Good has followed bad." Giving Mary a hug she said, "My dear, you will never know how much I have grieved, missed you, wept for Antonio and all that has happened. God has answered my prayers, although of course I wish poor Antonio had not died. But let us be happy."

"I cannot forget the past, Mother," said Mary. "And find it hard to forgive Father. The Lord's prayer says 'forgive us our trespasses as we forgive them who trespass against us', but it is hard to do. However, Father has asked for forgiveness and this I must do. I loved Antonio and he was a wonderful husband, but I cannot bring him back. If I could I would, but he is in heaven and guarded by the angels. Lord Clements is kind and I feel that I shall be happy with him."

"My dear, I am sure so," replied Georgina, and kissed Mary fondly on the cheek.

CHAPTER 28

Events moved on. Lord Clements, true to his word, called frequently at Thornton House to take Mary for rides and to see his manor at Thropston. Mr Wakefield, guilty of his past behaviour, gave Mary a generous dowry of five thousand pounds.

Meanwhile, the work to restore the stables was completed and true to his word Lord Derby gave the head groom £500, which enabled him to buy outright a small thatched cottage that was for sale with a large piece of land surrounding it. He was able to arrange for a stable to be built on his own land and purchased two horses for himself. He still continued with his employment with Lord Derby, however, but knew for sure that his future was secure. The head stableman with the name of Dickson was unmarried but had been secretly courting Gladys, Lady Derby's maid. He felt that he could soon propose, but knew that she too would wish to continue to work for Lord Derby. With their combined wages he felt that they too could employ a stable boy-cum-house boy, and a servant to help within the cottage.

Mr Burstow, when sentenced in court, agreed to pay the considerable fine, which Lord Derby insisted should be set aside for a school to be built locally for the village children, many of whom could neither read nor write. Nancy herself was to interview staff when the building was completed.

Mr and Mrs Burstow decided to sell their property and together with Isobelle and Thomas emigrated to America. They were not heard from again.

To Nancy's joy she found that she was again pregnant and was secretly hoping that she would give birth to a baby girl. She loved Emily and Anna, but they would eventually make their debut and be wed themselves. This pregnancy did not progress so well, however, as it had with Edmund. Despite still teaching the girls sewing, art, music, etiquette and deportment, she was often unable to do all the daily tasks as she had such dreadful nausea.

Doctor Fairfax was called in, and although he prescribed Laudanum, and stated that he felt sure the sickness would abate, it did not, and Nancy began to feel very concerned as did Lord Derby.

Mary and Lord Clements married in the Church at Merridon and gained many friends of Nancy and Lord Derby and they were amongst the guests. Lord and Lady Hastings were there of course. Mr Wakefield gave Mary away and although it was a second marriage, she wore a white gown trimmed with pink roses. She looked young and revitalised and was happy to spend her honeymoon at Thropston Manor. Georgina arranged a wonderful reception for the couple at Thornton House and the carriage finally taking them back to Thropston Manor was bedecked with white ribbon.

As they arrived on the drive at the front entrance, all the staff were lined up to greet her. She had of course met some already when visiting the manor, but it was rather overwhelming to see everyone employed lined up to greet her.

There were too many for Lord Clements to introduce but he introduced some whom she had previously met and others that she had not. The staff abandoned all etiquette and waved and clapped as she and Lord Clements entered the manor. Both the twins and Lord Clements' sons had accompanied them throughout, and they all looked very handsome in their finery. They seemed very happy for their parents' union with no rivalries or jealousies between them.

Lord Clements thanked the staff and stated that there would be wine and ale within, which he had secretly planned with his housekeeper Mrs Durban.

Lord Clements had arranged for his new wife's rooms and his adjoining room to be in the East Wing of the house instead of the West Wing that he had previously shared with his late wife.

He had asked Mary about décor, but she replied that she wished it to be a surprise. And surprise it was. The main bedroom had a sumptuous four poster bed, with curved oak posts. The curtaining was blue velvet. The windows looked out onto the great park where glistening water could be seen in the distance. The carpet was a luxurious blue and the furniture of deep mahogany. The whole room was decorated with gold covered wallpaper and all cushions and covers were also in gold. There was a gold chaise longue, and chairs which were also covered in gold satin.

Mary could not take it all in. Her father's house was more plainly furnished. Very good quality of course, as he was a rich man, but nothing as elegant as this room. To her joy she also found that a bathroom had been added when she opened one door.

Lord Clements entered and asked if she was pleased.

"I am overjoyed," Mary replied. "Thank you so much. All within this room is perfect."

"You too are perfect," Lord Clements replied.

Despite having his own room, they slept in the main bedroom together that night. Mary had loved Antonio deeply and of course had borne Nancy and the twins. Antonio had been a passionate lover, but years had passed. Mary felt contentment in Lord Clements' arms and felt safe and secure. They coupled together and both felt at peace with the world.

Nancy had of course attended the wedding despite her pregnancy and feeling uncomfortable. She had had a new gown made of dark blue with pale blue trimmings and a pale blue bonnet.

After the couple had left and guests departed from Thornton House, Nancy said that she felt the need to return home quickly. Lord Derby arranged this immediately, but upon arriving at Fairstow House, Nancy realised that she was bleeding. Hastily Doctor Fairfax was called but was sorry to say that Nancy was having a miscarriage. Nancy was in great pain and Doctor Fairfax called in a nurse to help as well.

Nancy bled a great deal and Doctor Fairfax was gravely concerned. He told Lord Derby who was almost demented, to prepare for the worst. The whole household was almost in silence as the malformed foetus was carried away and it was obvious that Nancy's life hung in the balance.

Doctor Fairfax did not return home, nor the newly called in nurse, but stayed in the room with Nancy until morning. As the sun rose, Doctor Fairfax could see that she had turned a corner and would live. The nurse cleaned up all that was necessary and Gladys put a new nightgown upon Nancy. She was now conscious but wept upon hearing that she was no longer pregnant. Doctor Fairfax had to tell her that it was highly improbable that she could bear another child. When Lord Derby heard this news, he was saddened but deeply grateful that the woman he loved lived.

CHAPTER 29

It was some days before Nancy could be up and resume her life, albeit gently and carefully. She spent more time with Edmund and of course Emily and Anna.

The new village school was unfinished as yet, but she asked the steward to advertise for a superior governess, a lady of quality who could put the final touches to the girl's education and prepare them for their debut into society later.

There was another catastrophe, however, as Anna, the younger of the girls, fell from her horse and severely broke her arm in two places. Again, Doctor Fairfax was called in to set the arm, and to check frequently that all was going well. Lord Derby felt that he should transport his family to a hunting lodge he had in Lockerbie, and suggested this to Nancy. Anna still had her arm in plaster and Nancy felt that such a move would only be possible when the arm had finally healed and the plaster removed. She was also concerned that such a journey would be inadvisable for baby Edmund, and for the first time, there appeared to be a tension between the two of them.

Lord Derby was feeling fraught and tired himself. He had endured the hostility of the Burstows. Now the trauma of the burned stables to endure. He had nearly died a thousand deaths when Nancy had her miscarriage and was so ill; he felt dispirited and drained.

This apathy spread through the household. It was apparent that his spirits needed lifting, as did those of his wife. The young nurse who had been brought in to tend Nancy was also still coming in to see to Anna. No lady had been found suitable as yet to give town bronze to the two girls, and this had in fact been set back by the break to Anna's arm.

The young nurse appeared to have some sort of 'crush' on Lord Derby and he had to admit that she was lovely to look upon, and he did in fact, in his lowered state of mind, feel flattered. There had been no sexual activity between Nancy and himself for some time due to her feeling generally unwell, and then of course the miscarriage. He had never taken a mistress as did many of his station, as he gathered that many became too demanding, also of course often expensive. He was later then too involved with his brother and wife's deaths and his concern for his nieces. The nurse seemed to invent situations in which to converse and even after Doctor Fairfax had removed Anna's plaster, still said that it was her duty to look in frequently on Anna and of course Nancy. Doctor Fairfax himself thought that this was excellent, and knew that Lord Derby would willingly pay the extra money for the nurse's administrations when the bill from the surgery was sent. Doctor Fairfax himself had no idea that the nurse was so delighted with these arrangements.

Nancy began to do some teaching with the girls as no suitable candidate had come forward from Rowan's Agency and there had been no response from two advertisements that had been placed in the local paper. Lord Derby had written to his sister, Cassandra, about the problem, and she had replied that she had a distant cousin, aged forty, who was well educated, but had had no wish for marriage and still lived with her elderly parents, who now had a permanent carer living in. She was now no longer required and could possibly be suitable. She herself had been presented at court and knew all the correct etiquette necessary for the future of the children.

Lord Derby had replied that with his sister's recommendation, he felt that this lady could be employed as soon as convenient. He felt that to supervise the girls and to rear Edmund, apart from checking menus and still be the main person in charge of all the household, this was sufficient strain upon Nancy's health.

The nurse, meanwhile, was still visiting each day, to check Nancy's pulse, and now to massage Anna's arm. Whenever she passed Lord Derby she gave him a brilliant smile and one day she was about to visit him in the library when she saw Lord Derby had caught his hand in the door of a bookcase. Without hesitation, or sending for a servant, she fetched cold water herself and gently bathed the hand and then massaged it.

The pain eased from Lord Derby's hand and he made to withdraw it. The nurse, however, did not release it and softly kissed the back of his hand. She then began to stroke his arm with a light feathery motion. Lord Derby felt himself responding to this almost against his will. He found himself drawing the nurse towards himself and gently kissed her. The nurse abandoned any thoughts of further bathing or massaging the hand, and throwing her arms around Lord Derby's neck, kissed him passionately. Lord Derby felt himself groping for her breast beneath her uniform and the nurse moaned with pleasure.

Unfortunately, at that moment, Mason opened the door and Nancy entered with the girls. Viewing the scene, Nancy immediately indicated that Mason should close the door and ushered the girls back upstairs to the school room. Baby Edmund was, of course, being attended to by the nurse, Betty.

Nancy gave the girls some writing to copy then went to her room. She was totally heartbroken. She had been so convinced that the love between Lord Derby and herself was enduring and had never thought for one moment that he would betray her.

She knew that Isobelle had tried with the help of the family to tempt him, and he had even tried to find a wife at the ball, but his love for Nancy had overridden all the efforts various girls' mamas had made to tempt him to marriage. He had chosen her above all others and yet she had just seen him in what appeared to be a passionate kiss with the nurse.

CHAPTER 30

Nancy did not know what to do. She had heard of the possibility of a distant cousin of Cassandra coming to supplement the time that she could now give to the girls and wondered if that had made her less important to Lord Derby. But then she had given birth to a son, who was now heir to Fairstow. Surely that was very important to him, she mused. But then perhaps the fact that there may be no more children of his own flesh and blood had turned him against her. She was in a quandary as to what she should do. She certainly didn't wish to spoil her mother's happiness by rushing to Thropston and certainly would not go to her grandparents' home, Thornton.

The girls were happily in the school room and she had managed herself to close the door before Mason could do so, before they could see Lord Derby and the nurse. Luckily they had been a few steps behind her. Baby Edmund was safely with Betty. She threw on a cloak and exited down the stairs usually used by the servants. Harrison was on duty by the main door, but she slipped out of the servants' entrance and just started walking. She was approaching the lake and remembered all the trouble the Burstow boy had caused. She carried on around the lake and then just sat down under a tree and wept.

Meanwhile, Lord Derby was totally horrified at his weak moment, but could not totally blame the nurse, only condemn himself for his utter stupidity.

"My dear," he said to the nurse. "You have done an excellent job in looking after both my wife and daughter, but I shall tell Doctor Fairfax that we are no longer in need of your services. Please leave now and ask Doctor Fairfax to send on his account."

The nurse of course realised that Nancy must have seen them and also realised that there was no future for her with Lord Derby.

"I understand, my Lord," she said. "I will gather my things together and leave at once. I am sorry that my emotions overcame me, but we cannot help it when love comes knocking at the door. I know that Lady Derby has been unwell for some time and perhaps hoped that I could at least have become your mistress."

Lord Derby gasped. "Good heavens, girl, whatever are you saying. You are a nurse albeit young, but of good repute, otherwise Doctor Fairfax would not employ you. You should not have even had such wicked thoughts, but I am to blame as I am older and should have been wiser. What you thought could never have been, it was just a transient error on my part."

The nurse smiled sadly. "I suppose we can all have dreams," she said as she moved towards the door. "I may be young, but I do not think I shall ever feel the same towards another man." So saying she left.

Lord Derby was puzzled. He would not insult her by discussing it with Doctor Fairfax. He knew the reason for his misdemeanour – low spirits and a lack of his conjugal relations with Nancy, but what about the nurse? Perhaps she had had too little affection in her life. Whatever the reasons for the debacle, he must find Nancy to try to make amends if he could.

He rang for Gladys.

"Is my wife in her room?" he enquired.

"No, my Lord, I just knocked to see if there was anything required, but there was no answer. I opened the door and the room was empty."

Lord Derby began to feel full of trepidation. He rang for Mason.

"Have you seen my Lady?" he enquired.

"I believe she was seen by a servant walking towards the lake, my Lord. I was just about to inform Gladys and we are going to follow her to ensure that all is well. We were concerned as there appeared to be no maid at all with her."

Lord Derby was now deeply troubled.

"Go after my Lady as fast as you are able. I will fetch Persephone and ride bareback in the direction at once."

Mason and Gladys set out, but unfortunately went to the right of the lake, whereas Lady Derby had walked to the left. Very shortly Lord Derby thundered up on Persephone, with no saddle or equipment.

CHAPTER 31

Lord Derby leaped down from the horse and knew that it would stay. He began to search frantically. At last he found Nancy, still sobbing.

"My dear! My dear! You must know that I love you beyond everything. You are my sun, moon and stars, and have made my life complete again after the death of my brother and sister-in-law. It was nothing, my dear. Nothing. The nurse was infatuated (she has now left forever), and it was just one moment of madness. Please, please my dear, forgive what was just stupidity."

Nancy looked at him and could see that he was totally distraught.

"I may not be able to bear another child," she whispered.

"Unimportant. I love my son, of course, but even if you had been barren I would still have loved and married you. We have Emily and Anna, and I was overwhelmed then for your love and kindness to them. Everything will soon be as it was as your health is improving every day. It was a grief to lose the baby, but sadly these things happen. Let us be strong together, my dear."

Nancy loved her husband and knew that recent events hadn't helped their relationship. She decided to try to forget the incident as if it had never happened.

She rose from the grass where she had been crouching. Lord Derby shouted loudly, "I have my Lady here."

Mason and Gladys heard this and turned. Lord Derby swept Nancy up into his arms onto the bare back of Persephone, still patiently waiting, and they galloped back to the house.

Lord Derby left Persephone to the groom who had run up at once, and carried Nancy up the staircase to her room. He gently disrobed her himself and placed her under the linen sheets edged with lace. He himself remained fully clothed, and lying on top of the bed, put his arms around her and just held her.

"I love you, Nancy Derby," he whispered. "And I always will."

When Gladys knocked at the door Lord Derby rose and ushered her away. He returned to Nancy, who had fallen asleep after all the trauma. Lord Derby still remained fully clothed on top of the counterpane and cuddled his wife's head to his breast.

Nancy smiled in her sleep and Lord Derby knew that the terrible moment had passed.

CHAPTER 32

Cassandra's relative, Clara, duly arrived and proved to be a blessing. She was high born, and therefore from her demeanour and manner, was respected by all the staff. She was an intelligent woman and did not intrude upon the relationship between Emily, Anna and Nancy. Nancy still did a little teaching with the children, when Clara had time to herself, but the majority of lessons were now with Clara. Baby Edmund seemed to grow rapidly, and was soon toddling around the household. He managed the staircase at the age of one and a half and was beginning to utter words. Nancy and Maximillian had of course resumed their married life together and the traumatic incident with the nurse was never ever again mentioned.

Emily and Anna still had some time to go before being presented at Court, but Clara had also really taken them under her wing, and Nancy and Maximillian knew that they would be most popular when the time was right. So it was Clara who encouraged Lord Derby to invite the daughters of local gentry of a similar age to the house, so that they could fully develop their roles of life and maybe society. Nancy had taught both girls the pianoforte, and they could now play pieces such as Chopin and Beethoven.

Clara suggested that they invite some neighbours to a soiree at which Emily and Anna could play. Nancy (reluctantly) was persuaded to play herself.

Mrs Chapman organised a lovely spread of food in the music salon, which of course had a Steinway Grand Pianoforte upon which Nancy had taught the children.

Thirty neighbours arrived by invitation including of course Mary and her new husband Lord Clements, Lord and Lady Hastings, and even Cassandra and her husband Mr Fanshaw. (They of course stayed for several nights.)

Everyone was delighted with the girl's playing; Anna played a simple Gavotte, but Emily played Chopin's waltz in C minor. This was greeted with rapturous applause.

Nancy herself played several Sonatinas by Clementir and Lord Derby beamed with pride.

He came up to Nancy, holding baby (now not so much a baby but a little man) Edmund by the hand. He kissed Nancy on the cheek and putting his arm around Anna and then Emily, addressed the audience.

"I hope you have enjoyed our concert," he said. "But I must say it cannot match the joy that I have with my family, Emily, Anna, Edmund and of course my greatest treasure, my wife Nancy."

He then added, "I must also thank Clara, my sister's relation, through marriage, who suggested such an occasion."

Everyone of course clapped loudly.

The village school was now completed and Nancy found an excellent teacher who could live in one of their cottages on the estate, to teach both boys and girls. At first only six children attended. Some villagers didn't hold with education and the rich of course either had tutors and governesses or went away to school. As the six children progressed with reading and writing, gradually any antipathy to the new school melted away, and eventually other children were allowed into the school.

At one time there were twenty-four children in the school and Lord Derby, using the money fined from Mr Burstow, provided excellent desks in the beginning and books for reading and writing. Nancy was delighted because she remembered how she herself had prospered at her village school with Mrs Higgs. Despite all her obligations she asked Lord Derby to provide a piano in the school and once a week she herself, like Mrs Higgs, who had so helped her, helped several children to success.

Nancy felt that her life had turned full circle and realised how fortunate she had been, despite Mr Wakefield's narrow-minded behaviour, she had learned, through hardship to appreciate all the joys that life could offer.

Lord and Lady Derby had no more children, but Edmund had a tutor and went on eventually to Oxford, as had James and John, Mary's sons. The girls had, in time, been presented at court, attended balls in London and Bath, and both made very happy marriages. Emily to a Lord Johnson and Anna to a Lord Grantham. Clara retired to a cottage on Lord Derby's estate and enjoyed herself painting landscapes.

Clara's life was complete. She attended chapel regularly and to everyone's delight formed an attachment to the still unmarried chaplain. As Clara had been so happy in her cottage, they married, and decided to forsake any church accommodation, but to live together in the cottage. The chaplain still, however, continued with his duties and they were both very happy together.

Lord and Lady Derby stayed in love and were loved and respected by both villagers and neighbours. Lord Derby rented out his hunting lodge, but kept it maintained where necessary in order that Edmund may himself wish to use it in the future.

Nancy pondered over her life and again decided that the hardship they had endured had made them all feel at one with those in hardship, and they all helped where it was needed.

Nancy looked at her husband and smiled as he dozed by the fire. Her dream to become a governess had indeed reaped many rewards.

DREAMS

We dream for what we wish for
Our thoughts soar like the wings of a dove,
We dream and hope for ever,
As we gaze to heaven above.

How much longing is there
In our every sleeping thought?
How much we desire and pray,
That all will not come to nought?

Life is full of turbulence,
A pattern like mountain slopes,
But when we dream all fades away,
And dreams are full of hopes.

A dream is like a whisper,
That floats into one's brain,
The whispers reflect on wishes,
That makes everything right again.

We see loved ones gone but there,
They return to us once more,

But when we wake they fade away,
But we have seen them that is sure.

May our dreams return we plead,
May they refresh our weary soul,
May they fleetly give us joy,
And make us truly whole.

DEL 2023